Carl Weber's Kingpins:

The Girls of South Beach

Carl Weber's Kingpins:

The Girls of South Beach

Treasure Hernandez

www.urbanbooks.net

Urban Books, LLC
300 Farmingdale Road, N.Y.-Route 109
Farmingdale, NY 11735

Carl Weber's Kingpins: The Girls of South Beach
Copyright © 2021 Treasure Hernandez

ISBN 13: 978-1-64556-146-0
ISBN 10: 1-64556-146-1

First Trade Paperback Printing February 2021
Printed in the United States of America

10 9 8 7 6 5 4 3 2 1

This is a work of fiction. Any references or similarities to actual events, real people, living or dead, or to real locales are intended to give the novel a sense of reality. Any similarity in other names, characters, places, and incidents is entirely coincidental.

Distributed by Kensington Publishing Corp.
Submit Orders to:
Customer Service
400 Hahn Road
Westminster, MD 21157-4627
Phone: 1-800-733-3000
Fax: 1-800-659-2436

Carl Weber's Kingpins:

The Girls of South Beach

Treasure Hernandez

Chapter 1

Now every little thing that we do
Should be between me and you
The freaky things that we do
Let's keep between me and you

"Babyyy!"

Anissa Burke spun around from where she stood in front of the full-length mirror and saw that her cousin Brynn had entered the bedroom they shared. She grinned at Brynn and turned down the music just as Ja Rule began to rap his verse. It was an old song, but it was still her jam and always put her in a good mood right before she went on a job.

"Titty check," Anissa said, putting her arms up and jumping up and down in her little black dress. A titty check was something they did to make sure that during a job, if they had to fight or even run from the police, their breasts would stay in place no matter what. After a few hard jumps, she looked down and was pleased her double-Ds were still in place.

"Titties checked," Brynn noted and eyed the dress enviously. "That dress is super cute on your frame. I knew I should have snatched it up when we were in the mall."

"Girl, you act like you won't ever be able to wear it. What's mine is yours, remember?"

"Yeah, yeah." Brynn rolled her eyes with a small smirk. "Just don't get any cum on it tonight. How does this red jumpsuit look? Is my ass sitting or what?"

Brynn used her hip to bump Anissa to the side so that she could get a clear view of herself in the mirror. The red really made her plump bottom look like an apple. Anissa observed her big cousin, and as always, she was in awe of her beauty. Brynn had smooth, peanut-buttery skin, and her Jamaican roots showed in her voluptuous shape. She had perky breasts, a slim waist, and a fat ass. She was four years older than Anissa, at 28, but she didn't look a year over 21. The two of them always kept their hair laid, and that night they opted for jet-black wigs. Brynn's was cut in a blunt Chinese bob with bangs, while Anissa's was twenty-two inches with a middle part.

"You know it's sitting," Anissa answered her cousin's question. "Anyways, what did you say these clowns do for a living again?"

"My date is a lawyer, and yours is some kind of foot doctor."

"Foot doctor?" Anissa made a face.

"You won't be making that ugly face when that money is in your hand at the end of the night," Brynn told her with a sly smile.

"Shiiiit, you're right about that!"

Anissa went over to the brown Birkin bag on the king-sized bed and pulled out a nude lip gloss that would go well with her golden skin. After she put some on, she rubbed her lips together and glanced over Brynn's shoulder to see her reflection in the mirror.

"Bitch, when are we going to get out of this woman's house?" she asked and put her lip gloss back where she got it. "We've been sharing this room for a year now. I be feeling like I barely have room to breathe."

"We said we would leave and get our own house when we stacked up a hundred K each," Brynn reminded her. "A goal is a goal. We just need to be consistent in turning these tricks and stop spending the money we make so frivolously."

Anissa sighed deeply and looked around the bedroom. It was nice, but she was ready for her surroundings to match the bad bitch she was on the inside. A beachfront home with the perfect view of the water would do her heart some good. The thought of having that one day was what kept her going. However, temporarily she would have to settle for the room they rented from a woman they called Miss Mandy, who, by the way, never missed a beat to remind them that they were in *her* house. It was annoying, but Brynn was right—a goal was a goal.

Anissa had been working as a high-priced escort with Brynn for the past year and a half. She'd moved to Miami Beach, Florida, from Atlanta after her mother, Diana, died from an overdose on a bad fix. Diana didn't have life insurance, so Anissa had to spend her entire savings to bury her. After that, she planned on staying in Georgia and keeping her low-paying CNA job to stack back up. However, when Brynn told her she could come stay with her, she jumped at the opportunity to jet to Florida. Anissa knew what Brynn did for work, and at first, she wasn't for it, but she changed her mind after seeing Brynn's lifestyle and all the things she was able to afford. Anissa allowed herself to be taught the game.

Brynn showed her how to walk, how to talk, and how to pinpoint the highest-paid man in the room just by his choice of cufflinks. The most important thing that Brynn taught her, however, was to always have an escape plan with that kind of work. She told Anissa that they couldn't turn tricks forever and that they should always want more out of life, which was why they had a savings goal. The moment they both had $100,000 saved up, they were going to be out of the game. Brynn wanted to open her own hair salon while Anissa wanted to start her own online fashion boutique.

"Shit. We have to go," Brynn said, checking the time.

The wooden clock on the wall read ten minutes before nine, making the young women put pep in their step. They were supposed to meet their dates by ten o'clock at a place that was forty-five minutes away. Anissa grabbed the silver clutch she would be carrying for the night and followed Brynn out of the room.

"Don't forget to lock the door," Anissa told Brynn, glancing down the hallway at Miss Mandy's closed bedroom door. "I don't want Miss Nosy to be all in our shit."

"That lady knows better than to step foot in this room," Brynn said, but still she pulled her key out and locked both locks on the bedroom door. "Okay, let's go."

Their heels clicked and clacked down the wooden stairs as they made their way to the front door. Once out of the house, they decided taking Brynn's black G-Wagen over Anissa's Audi would be a better choice. One of her tricks had gotten it for Brynn as a gift a while back, and it was her pride and joy. Anissa got in on the passenger side and instantly opened the glove compartment. She knew that was where her cousin hid the liquor if she had any.

"Ugh," she groaned and pulled out a pint of Hennessy. "I hate dark."

"Well, take it or leave it, because we won't have time to stop anywhere and grab anything else," Brynn said after she too was in the vehicle.

"Fuck it," Anissa said and unscrewed the top. She put the bottle to her lips and took a large swig from it, making a face as it went down. "Whew!"

"That's that shit that puts hair on your chest!" Brynn laughed and pulled away from the curb. "Here, give me some."

Anissa gladly passed her the bottle from hell and leaned back in her seat to wait for her buzz to kick in. She liked having some of the edge off when they went on dates. It helped her to not be so uptight with her clients.

After Brynn was done with the bottle, she put it back in the glove box and connected her phone to the Bluetooth in the car. Suddenly Moneybagg Yo's voice blared from the speakers, and Anissa instantly sat back up, getting hype. Her body rocked side to side, and she popped her bottom to the beat. She loved R&B, but there was just something about trap music that spoke to her soul. She and Brynn vibed out the entire ride to the meeting spot, singing and rapping whatever song was playing. When the G-Wagen finally pulled up to the address they were given, Anissa saw that they were in front of a tall residential skyscraper that said DYNASTY LOFTS.

"They said we can get a parking pass and pull into the parking garage, but I'm going to park on the street just to be on the safe side," Brynn said and did a U-turn in the middle of the street to park on the other side of it. "I've only gone on two dates with this muhfucka. Make sure you have your blade on you just in case."

"I never leave without it," Anissa said and shook her clutch slightly.

"I taught you well," Brynn noted and sprayed herself with some perfume from her armrest. "All right, let's get in there before they think we stood them up."

They got out of the car and crossed the street when there was a break in traffic, but even with cars coming, they didn't rush. The cars coming their way slowed down respectfully, and Anissa heard a whistle come from a BMW.

"You ladies are looking magnificent tonight! Which one of you wants to be my wife?"

She smiled without looking at the car and whipped her hair over her shoulders as she kept walking. One of Brynn's rules of being an escort was to always carry themselves as ladies with class. Not only that, but always require those around them to treat them as such. When they reached the tall glass doors, the doorman hurried to open one of them so that they could walk through.

"Thank you, handsome." Brynn winked at him.

"You're welcome, ma'am," he said, stumbling over his words.

As they made their way to the elevator, Anissa could feel his eyes on them the entire time. When they were in the elevator, Brynn pressed the button for the third floor, and Anissa checked her teeth with the camera on her phone. They were white, and there was nothing stuck in them.

"I was hoping we would be at a restaurant tonight," she pouted. "I didn't eat a thing before we left."

"If they don't have anything there, we'll make them order us something," Brynn assured her.

Ding! The door opened, and Anissa let her cousin lead the way since she seemed to know where they were going. The doors in the long hallway were spaced quite a distance apart, and the two of them stopped when they reached the last one on the right. Brynn knocked on the door, and within seconds it swung open. Standing in the doorway, smiling big, was a handsome white man with sandy brown hair. He was fit and looked to be in his mid-thirties. Anissa took notice of the wedding ring on his finger but didn't think too much about it. Most of her tricks were married or had long-term girlfriends. As long as their money spent, she didn't care if they had five wives.

"Well, if it isn't my new favorite girl in the whole world. Glad you could make it, Desire," he said, calling her by her fake name.

"Thank you for inviting me, Daniel," Brynn said seductively. "But I would be even more thankful if you invited us in."

"How rude of me," Daniel said and stepped out of the way. "Come in."

When they walked through the doorway, a gust of cool air hit Anissa's skin. It smelled like hot wings, and her eyes went right to the island in the open kitchen. Sure enough, there was a big plate of hot wings, celery, and fries. Not a five-star meal, but she would gladly take it.

"And who is your friend?" Daniel asked, and she turned her attention back to him.

"This is Genie, the girl I told you I would be bringing for your friend," Brynn told him and looked over his shoulder around the loft. "Where is he?"

"Right here!" a voice sounded, coming down from the spiral staircase. "I apologize. I was just in the bathroom."

Anissa was pleased that he too was handsome and had a nice build. He, however, was blond with blue eyes. Both men were dressed in dress slacks and nice button-ups. Anissa's date had the top two buttons of his shirt undone, giving them all a peek at his broad chest.

"I'm Pete," he said and shot her a dazzling white smile with a hand out.

"Hi, Pete, I'm—"

"Genie, I heard. And I must say, the name suits you," he said and looked her up and down, clearly impressed. "Are you hungry?"

"Starving," Anissa said, and he held his hand out.

She took it and let him lead her into the large kitchen area. Once there, he handed her a glass and opened a brand-new bottle of champagne. After pouring some in her glass, he poured some for himself.

"We wanted to take you ladies out for a nice dinner," Daniel said, bringing Brynn into the kitchen as well. "However, Pete here was worried someone who knew his wife would spot him. See, this is his first time."

"What? We have a first-timer?" Anissa teased Pete. "Well, I guess we'll have to make tonight extra special for you then."

"I'm hoping so," Pete said.

"But first a girl must eat," Anissa said with a giggle. The Hennessy she'd drunk in the car had made her hungrier than she already was. Although she could have scarfed down ten wings, she settled for half that and some celery. When she was done, she let Pete lead her upstairs to one of the bedrooms, and he shut the door behind them. He'd grabbed another bottle of champagne, and it looked like the night would be one of the easier ones. She still watched him closely with the bottle of champagne because she would be damned before she got drugged. He poured another glass of champagne, just one, and held it out to her before sitting on the soft comforter on top of the king-sized bed.

"Make yourself comfortable," he said and motioned for her to sit next to him.

"Don't mind if I do," Anissa said, obliging him with a smile.

"So, tell me about yourself. Where does the name Genie come from?"

"My name is Genie because I'm known for making wishes come true," she said, sticking her tongue out slightly before her lips met the rim of her wineglass. She downed the liquid and placed the glass on the nightstand beside the bed. "But me telling you about myself isn't how this works. I want to know about you, Pete."

"So, you can make my wishes come true?"

"See? You're a quick study. I like that," she said and placed a hand on his leg. "Who exactly *is* Pete?"

"That's a good question. I feel like although I'm thirty-nine years old, I'm still figuring that out."

"Then let's start with the basics."

"Okay," Pete said and cleared his throat. "Well, I am a podiatrist and have been for the past ten years. I'm also married. Daniel mentioned my wife."

"And I peeped your ring," Anissa told him and then waved a hand around the room. "If you're married, and so is your friend, what is this? Some type of hideaway man cave?"

"Something like that," Pete said with a sheepish grin. "Listen, I'm all for doing whatever tonight, but—"

"Leave everything in this room," Anissa finished for him with a giggle. "You don't have to tell me that, but I hope you remember that advice once you've tasted me. I don't like stalkers. Do you have kids?"

"Three. Two boys and one girl."

"Do you love your wife?"

"Very much so."

"Then why are you here?" Anissa asked and stood up.

There wasn't any music playing, but that didn't matter to her. Her buzz had her feeling herself, and her body needed to move. In front of him, she began to dance slowly and seductively. She turned around so that he could get a perfect view of her round bottom, and she rubbed her hips with her hands. Looking back at him, she saw that Pete's eyes were on her as if he were in a trance.

"Hmm? Why am I here, Pete?"

"Be . . . because I just need a little bit more excitement in the bedroom," he told her.

"A little bit? If that's all you want, I'm the wrong girl for you, because I don't do 'little.' Everything I do, I do it big."

On the word "big," Anissa bent over and touched her ankles. She felt her dress hike up and knew that Pete was looking dead at her exposed kitty cat. She usually didn't wear panties, and that night was no different. She twirled her bottom a few times before standing back up and turning to face him. His breathing had gotten shallow, and by the bulge in his pants, she could tell that he enjoyed her little show. She almost laughed at how easy it was, but she was enjoying being in control too much. She straddled him and ground her crotch into his while leaning into him.

"Tell me what you like," she asked softly in his ear. "Do you want to dominate me, or do you want me to be in control?"

"I . . . I don't know," he answered honestly. "I just want to . . . I just want to—"

"You just want to what?"

"I just want to fuck you."

"All right," Anissa said and stood up straight. "You're aware of my fee and requirements, correct?"

"Yes, the money is in the nightstand," Pete told her and pointed, "along with my recent doctor's papers. I'm as clean as a whistle."

Anissa opened the nightstand, and sure enough there was a stack of fresh hundred-dollar bills on top of his test results as well as a pack of condoms. She looked thoroughly over the notes and counted the money to make sure everything was good.

"My fee is five thousand dollars. There is six thousand here," she told him.

"If it's as good as I'm hoping, consider that your tip," Pete said, unbuttoning his shirt.

"Oh, it will be," Anissa said with a wide grin.

The loud snoring inside the bedroom was what signaled Anissa that it was time to go. Pete lay sprawled on the disheveled bed, completely naked and with a filled condom halfway off his manhood. Genie had delivered to him every wish he commanded, and at the happy ending was a powerful orgasm that put him right to sleep.

She'd freshened up inside the adjoining bathroom before redressing and grabbing her money from the nightstand. It almost all didn't fit in her clutch, but with some force, she was able to attach the clasp. Before she left, she left her contact information so Pete could call her directly to set up another date. When she stepped out of the bedroom into the dimly lit loft, she saw that Brynn was already headed toward the stairs. They exchanged a look without saying anything to each other and made their way to the front door. Before exiting, Anissa piled some hot wings on a plate to take with her, and as soon as she got in the car, she devoured them. It didn't matter to her that they were cold. They were delicious all the same. When she was done, she leaned far back in her seat and watched the stars come and go as Brynn drove them home.

Chapter 2

"Bitch, I know you took it! Because it was here when I left last night!"

"Girl, you better watch ya fuckin' mouth talkin' to me like that!"

The sound of a heated argument made Anissa stir in her sleep. Normally she was a hard sleeper after a date, but the shouting invaded her dreams and forced her eyes to jerk open. She'd been buried deep under the covers of the bed she and Brynn shared, and when she tossed them over her head, she saw Brynn blocking the doorway so Miss Mandy couldn't get out. The older woman was still in her pajamas and had a head full of rollers. She kept trying to push past Brynn, but Brynn kept pushing her back. Confused, she sat up and rubbed her eyes.

"Cuz, what's going on?"

"This bitch got me for ten bands! That's what's going on."

"What?" Anissa asked, suddenly wide awake. "Ten bands?"

"Tennnn bandddsss," Brynn confirmed, clapping her hands together. "All my money was in my stash spot before I left. But when I went to add what I made last night, I could tell someone had been in my bag. And this morning, I don't think this ho knew we were home. I heard her fucking with the doorknob, so I opened the door and pulled her in here. And she ain't leaving until I get my money!"

Brynn kept her duffle bag of money hidden deep under the bed. Although it was out of public view, Anissa had always thought it wasn't a good place to hide so much money. She kept her money hidden in the wide bathroom vent since it didn't work. She kicked the covers off and went to their bathroom to check on her own paper. When she did, she saw that all her money was accounted for, minus the $6,000 still in her clutch.

"Are you sure you didn't miscalculate?" Anissa asked, coming out of the bathroom. "I mean, you locked the door before we left. How could she have gotten in?"

"I had sixty bands in there last night, and now I only have a little over fifty. I didn't miscalculate shit! And the only person here was this bitch."

"It was probably one of those filthy-ass men you get the money from in the first place!" Miss Mandy shouted. "Trifling hookers. I don't know why I even let you move in here anyways."

"Okay, everybody, calm down," Anissa said, trying to keep the situation from boiling over. She knew Brynn's temper could get out of control, and she didn't want it to get to that point. "Brynn, how could she have gotten in here to steal it in the first place?"

"The lock on that door is one she bought," Brynn said, putting two fingers in Miss Mandy's face. "It came with two sets of keys, and she only gave me one set when I moved in. The ones you have, Nissa, I had to get made. Ain't no telling how many times this ho done been up in here while I'm gone."

"Is that true?" Anissa asked and looked at Miss Mandy's wrinkled, stricken face.

The older woman had guilt written all over her, and Anissa wanted to smack fire from her herself. But she didn't. Instead, she nodded her head and walked to the door.

"Excuse me," she said calmly to Brynn.

"Where you going?"

"To check this ho's room for your money."

"You better stay the hell out of my room!" Miss Mandy screamed and tried to rush toward Anissa with raised fists.

"Bitch, I wish you would touch my cousin. I'll knock your head smooth the fuck off," Brynn threatened and jumped at Miss Mandy.

Miss Mandy stopped in her tracks, and Brynn let Anissa out the door. She went straight to Miss Mandy's room to search for the missing money. She didn't need to flip on the light, because the sunlight from the open window lit up the entire room. The first place Anissa checked was the closet. She did a thorough check, and although she didn't find the money, she found proof that Miss Mandy had in fact been in their room at least once before.

"I thought I lost this." Anissa smacked her lips and pulled down a red Gucci fanny pack she'd been convinced she'd misplaced. "This bitch got me for my Gucci!"

Upon looking some more, she noticed that wasn't the only possession that had been stolen. She found a Dior dress Brynn had torn their room up looking for, a Louis Vuitton phone case, and a few more designer items that both she and Brynn had given up looking for. The whole time they were down the hall.

"Well, ain't this about a bitch," Anissa said, shaking her head.

She placed the items under her arm and stepped out of the closet. Her eyes skimmed the room as she tried to think where she would hide something if she were Miss Mandy. Anissa's gaze fell on a trunk under the bedroom window, and she saw that the clasp was unfastened. She approached it and lifted the top. Sure enough, still wrapped in a rubber band was a roll of money. Shen knew it was Brynn's because she used red rubber bands on her bank rolls.

Anissa snatched it up and went back to their bedroom with all the items in tow. Brynn's eyes widened in anger when she saw the money in Anissa's hand, but her mouth dropped when she saw all the other things she came with. Miss Mandy, knowing she had been found out, looked terrified. She even took a few steps back.

"You thieving bitch!" Brynn shouted and raised her hand to strike the woman, but Anissa caught her arm.

"Nope. She's not worth catching a case over, Brynn."

"That's right, because if you place one hand on me, I'm gonna call the cops! Matter of fact, the second I'm out of this room I'm calling!"

"And telling them what? That you robbed me?" Brynn shouted.

"I'm gonna tell them that you two whores have been prostituting out of my house, and guess what? I bet they take *all* of that money!"

"How you gonna do that, Mandy Adelle Lawrence?" Brynn shocked everyone by calling Miss Mandy by her full government name. "Don't you have two outstanding traffic warrants?"

"How do you know that?"

"Bitch, do you think I would just move myself and all that cash into a place without some sort of leverage?" Brynn asked and looked at Miss Mandy as if she were crazy. "I did my research on you, and I knew you were all about making a quick buck when I gave you a fake name on my application. I know you didn't do any kind of background search. So go ahead, call the police. But I bet they won't find the girl you're talking about *if* they even let you get a word in before taking your ass to jail."

Miss Mandy inhaled deeply, and her eyes were as big as saucers as she realized her back was against the wall. She looked back and forth between the young women in front of her before letting out an angry shriek.

"I want the two of you out of my house before the day is up! Do you understand me? I want you out of here!"

"You don't have to tell us twice. I won't stay anywhere my money isn't safe," Brynn said and stepped aside, finally letting Miss Mandy out.

Brynn's words played over in Anissa's head, and she suddenly understood why Brynn said to only call each other "cuz" or "cousin" in the house. She never thought anything of it really since they were blood cousins. But now she knew it was because she didn't want Miss Mandy to know either of their real names.

When the woman was gone, Anissa sighed and fell on the bed. "Where are we gonna go?" she asked. "I would say a hotel, but not with all the shit we're gonna have to have in our cars. And what about your bed set?"

"She can keep the bed set." Brynn shrugged. "All we need to take with us are our clothes, shoes, and whatever personal items are in this ho. And you let me worry about where we're gonna rest our heads tonight. I brought you into this mess, so trust that big cuz is gonna get us out of it."

"All right."

The two of them got busy packing things up. The first things they grabbed were their duffle bags of money, then everything else. Whatever didn't fit in their luggage sets was thrown into trash bags. It only took about three hours for them to pack everything up and load it all into their vehicles.

On their way out of the house, Miss Mandy was standing by the open front door with her arms crossed. The rollers were still in her hair, but she had put on an emerald-colored robe over her nightclothes.

"Y'all better not have torn up that room," she sneered and held her hand out. "Give me my key. I don't want y'all coming back here."

"You want these keys?" Brynn asked and held the house keys up. "Fetch!"

Before Miss Mandy could snatch them from her, Brynn launched them somewhere outside.

"You raggedy heffa!" Miss Mandy ran outside to find where the keys had landed.

"Hopefully you can find them!" Brynn taunted, and Anissa cracked up as she watched Miss Mandy search feverishly for the keys. "Come on, Nissa. Fuck this bitch. We out! Just follow me. I'm about to make some phone calls."

Once again, Anissa did what her big cousin said. Getting in her car, she drove closely behind the G-Wagen. Her belly growled loudly, signaling that she was hungry and reminding her that she hadn't eaten a single thing since she'd awakened. She groaned as they passed several restaurants, because anything sounded good at the moment. Stopping at any of them, even in the drive-through, wouldn't be wise, however. Especially with the bag of money in the passenger's seat. Still, she hoped that they would get to where they were going fast. Anissa got the worst attitude when she was hungry.

To her surprise, the drive was relatively short. They started in Overtown and ended up in South Beach. Brynn pulled her car into the parking garage of a tall condominium and waved her hand out the window for Anissa to follow her.

"I know this bitch didn't schedule a date while we're supposed to be figuring out where we're going to be staying," Anissa said to herself. "I'll put my shit in storage for all this!"

She pulled her Audi into the garage and parked beside Brynn, but she didn't turn her car off. She rolled her window down so she could ask Brynn what they were doing there, but her cousin was on the phone. She had a big smile on her face, like someone had just told her something that made her very happy. When she disconnected the call, Brynn turned her car off and hopped out.

"Bitch!" she exclaimed excitedly, running to Anissa's window.

"Girl, what are we doing here?" Anissa asked. "Did you set up another date?"

"Nope," Brynn said with a grin. "That was one of my old tricks, Bill, on the phone though."

"Old tricks?"

"Girl, yeah. We don't get down anymore. He apparently grew a heart and decided to be faithful to his wife," Brynn said with a shrug. "He's still there whenever I need him though. He was a cool dude. He owns a condo here, the one we used to spend our time in. I asked him if I could crash in it until I find somewhere to stay, and guess what he said?"

"Yes?" Anissa assumed.

"Better than yes. He said it's mine and I can have it!" she squealed.

"Yours? What?" Anissa asked suspiciously.

"Bill was my very first client when *I* moved here from the A. He took care of me and was always good to me. He always told me whatever I need, ask him, and he'll make it happen. His wife doesn't know about this condo, and by him giving it to me, she'll never know. He said he'll come over with all the paperwork in the morning."

"And you trust him?"

"With my life," Brynn said without hesitation.

"He must be really rich."

"Rolling in dough," Brynn confirmed. "That's why his wife will never leave him. She signed a prenup. Now get the shit you can carry, and let's go. Oh, my God, Nissa! You're going to love this place."

The girls carried what they could the first go-round up to the tenth floor, and by the time they got there, Anissa was out of breath. Even though they'd used the elevator, it was still a long walk.

"How are we going to get in?" Anissa asked, looking at the door. There was no keyhole or spot for a fob, only a keypad with numbers.

Brynn pressed a combination of numbers, and on the last one, there was a click. She pushed the door open and grinned at Anissa. "The code is my birthday. He never changed it," she said.

The little breath Anissa had regained was taken when she got a look at the inside of the condo. Brynn had been right. She did love it, from the high-rise ceilings and wooden floors to the tall windows with the splendid view of the beach. The kitchen was open with a medium-sized granite island that had barstools scooted under it. The whole place was completely furnished and had a modern vibe about it.

"Wow," Anissa said, dropping her bags on the floor. "This is—"

"Ours," Brynn finished for her and grabbed her hand. "Come on, let me show you your room."

She dragged Anissa down a long, curved hallway to a huge bedroom. The view from inside it was amazing. They could see what seemed like the entire city from the window. Anissa also loved the way the sun hit every corner of the room. The queen bed already had a silver and white comforter set on it, but the closet and drawers were empty. Anissa was completely in awe, mainly because just the night before she had been thinking about how great it would be to have a place that matched the bad bitch inside. And now there she was, standing in it. She looked at her cousin and pointed to the bed.

"Brynn, before I fall out on that bed and scream my head off, are you sure this is where we're going to be staying?"

"Girl, it's ours. Bill is good people. If he says it's mine, it's mine. So, scream your head off and come on so we can get the rest of this shit! We need to go shopping for tonight."

"Tonight?" Anissa asked, racking her mind to make sure she wasn't forgetting about a scheduled date.

"We have to celebrate! And we can't do that without something new on our asses."

"Wait, didn't you *just* say we need to cut down on spending?"

"Don't use my words against me, ho," Brynn chastised playfully. "This is different. I'm feeling good. Out with the old, and in with the new. Fuck what they taught in school. It ain't what you know. It's who you put that good pussy on!"

As always, when Brynn and Anissa stepped out, they were among the flyest to do it. That night they decided to party in South Beach at a club called Blink. There were so many people dancing and drinking in the parking lot that one might have assumed that was where the party was. It was live, and the moment they stepped out at the valet, all eyes went straight to them. Brynn rocked a pink two-piece diamond-studded biker short set while Anissa sported a pair of short, distressed shorts and a lime green mock bikini top. Her abs put all the girls around her to shame. She had decided on wearing her loose, long, natural curls that night, and she knew she was a sight to see.

They skipped the line by passing the sea of people swarming the doorman to gain entry. Brynn winked at the big man, and he stepped out of their way so they could walk into the loud club. They ignored the usual catcalls being directed at them and didn't stop walking until they reached the bar.

"Okay! This bitch lit tonight!" Brynn yelled over Roddy Ricch's voice. She was leaned against the bar, peeping the scene with a satisfied look on her face. There was a lot of ass shaking and smacking going on, and she wanted to join the excitement. "I'm ready to get on the dance floor."

"What can I get you ladies to drink?" a handsome young bartender asked, approaching them. He rocked his hair in short twists, and his muscles were busting out of his button-up. His eyes didn't practice temperance as he looked them thirstily up and down. Anissa wondered which one of them he was screwing in his mind at that very second.

"Let me get a bottle of D'ussé," she told him, pointing at the bottle she wanted.

"Coming right up."

Within seconds he was back with their bottle, and she handed him a crisp hundred-dollar bill.

"Keep the change," Anissa told him with a wink, and he smiled big.

She opened the bottle and took a gulp. She and Brynn had pre-gamed before hitting the night scene, but she wasn't feeling it. She liked to drink until her lips were numb, and only then did she know she'd reached her level.

"Stop hogging the bottle! I'm tryin'a drive the boat!" Brynn exclaimed and held her mouth open.

"Ayyy!" Anissa hyped her as she poured the liquid without spilling a single drop.

Coincidentally, at that moment Megan Thee Stallion's song "Simon Says" began blaring through the speakers, and they knew it was time to make their way to the dance floor. When they did, they put on a show. They twerked until their backs hurt, and even then, they didn't stop. They quickly became the life of the party, and everyone wanted to be by them. Anissa saw so many phone lights on them and knew they would be on many Snapchats that night, but she didn't care. She was feeling good and looking good, and the D'ussé was having its way with her. A few men tried to dance with her, but she declined. She was just fine by herself. Brynn, on the other hand, had disappeared to the corner with some man. Her ass was all over his lap, grinding away.

When Jhené Aiko's song "Pussy Fairy" came on, it seemed as though everyone paired off except Anissa. She swayed her body to the beautiful melody and wound her hips with closed eyes.

"Now that I've got you right here, I won't let you down" She was into the song, singing the lyrics as she danced. When she opened her eyes, they fell on someone sitting across the dance floor on a stool at the bar. He was a fine caramel-complected man with a clean line up and soft sponge curls on his head. His eyes were on her, and as intensely as he was staring at her, she got the notion that he'd been watching her for a while. She batted her long eyelashes at him a few times before taking another swig from the bottle in her hands and turning her back on him. She continued dancing to the song, and once again was into it. Anissa didn't even feel someone come up to her from behind until she felt breath on the side of her face.

"I don't like when people turn their back on me," a seductive voice said in her ear.

Anissa felt chills down her spine, but the good kind. She glanced behind her and saw the man from the bar.

He was even finer close up and smelled delicious. He was a little over six feet tall, and even in her heels, Anissa barely stood to his shoulder. He rocked a Cubs jersey unbuttoned, exposing his muscular, tattooed chest. She bit her lip because he had the kind of face she liked: smooth, with not much facial hair. Just a thin mustache and a goatee.

"I was just vibing," she told him. "This is my song."

"Well, I came over here to see if I could vibe with you. But judging by the way you've been declining men all night, I'm sure that's gon' be a no, huh?"

"If you think that, why did you come over here?" Anissa asked and turned around fully to face him.

"Because you're the most beautiful woman in this club. I had to try," he said, shrugging his shoulders.

"Well, you're right. The answer probably would have been no. What's your name?"

"Huh?" he said and made a face like he couldn't hear her.

"What's your name?" Anissa asked a little louder.

"I can't hear you over the music," he said with a mischievous smile. "Can we take this conversation back over to the bar?"

"You think you're slick," Anissa said but couldn't help the small smile creeping to her lips.

"I mean, if I can't get a dance, can a man at least get some conversation?"

"Mmm, now you can hear me." Anissa rolled her eyes. "You're lucky my feet hurt."

She didn't wait for him to start walking before she went toward the barstool he had been sitting at. She took a seat beside it and set her bottle on the bar top. When he sat down, the two of them connected eyes and instantly began grinning.

"What you smiling for?" he asked.

"Because you still haven't told me your name."

"Damn! I just sat down," he joked. "You're a mean one, aren't you?"

"It depends on who's telling you about me."

"I see. Well, my name is Leon. What about you, beautiful?"

"I'm Anissa," she answered too fast and almost pinched herself. She never gave her real name when she was out at any club. She didn't know why it just slipped out like that.

"Anissa. I like that," Leon said with a genuine smile. He had a small gap between his otherwise perfectly straight teeth. He also had dimples. Those two things gave him character and made her stomach flutter a little bit. That and the fact that his gold bottom grill was gleaming in the strobe lights. "Well, it's nice to meet you, Anissa. Do you come here often?"

"I've been here once or twice," she told him.

"You aren't from here, are you?"

"How you figure that?"

"Your accent and that body. If I had to guess, I'd say Atlanta."

"And I would say you're a pretty good guesser."

"I fuck with Atlanta. It's like the black Hollywood up there. Every time I go, I seem to run into somebody famous. Be making me feel like a star myself."

"Yeah. I was in an episode of *Love & Hip Hop* a while back."

"So, you're a celebrity is what you're telling me?"

"Sure. If you call being an extra in the background celeb status. If you look at the scene close enough, you can almost make out my face clearly."

They shared a laugh, but Anissa cut hers short. She was flirting, definitely flirting. And she only did that with clients. Paying customers. Not random dudes at clubs. He might have been able to afford her rate, but by the way he was looking at her, she could tell he was the type to get attached. And that was something she didn't do. Not while she was still a working girl. She couldn't be loyal to a man while hopping in and out of bed with others, so for the time being, she chose to only be loyal to herself.

"I knew there was some humor behind that hard exterior," he said, charming her with another smile. "So, what made you move, and how long have you been up here? There are nothing but opportunities in the A for a girl like you."

"I usually don't tell people my business, but since I probably won't ever see you again, what the hell," Anissa sighed. "My mom died a little while back. A bad trip. When I found her, she had been dead for hours. So, I left and came here, and I've been here for a little over a year now."

"Damn, I'm sorry to hear about your moms. I know that shit wasn't easy."

"And how would you know?" Anissa asked, pursing her lips.

"Because I went through the same thing with my pops. He died a few years ago in the hospital. The nurse gave him too much morphine. It killed him. It was sad, but I was born and raised here. I ain't planning on leaving anytime soon. My roots and everything else are right here. Plus, he left everything to me when he died."

"I'm sorry," she said genuinely. "I didn't mean to assume you didn't understand how I felt. It's just that—"

"Most people don't."

"Exactly."

"Don't worry about it. Now that I've met you, I for sure don't have a reason to move. That is, unless you go back to Atlanta."

"Boy, you don't even know me like that," Anissa said, smacking her lips to prevent herself from smiling. "This is why I can't deal with niggas for real. Always tryin'a game somebody."

"Ain't nobody tryin'a game you, girl," Leon laughed. "I can just tell you're the type of girl I like. The type I need on my team."

"And what type is that?"

"Mean. Not easy to get to. Closed off. It means you can be loyal." He stared deeply into her eyes as he spoke every word.

"I'm not loyal to anybody but myself," she told him.

"And you're honest. I like that. A lot."

"All right! It's almost time to go on home, so I got one more song for y'all tonight!" the DJ said right before spinning the last song of the night.

It was Tank, "When We." Leon grabbed Anissa's hand softly to take her back to the dance floor, but she hesitated. He looked down at her with longing eyes.

"I don't know if I'll ever see you again, shawty. I just want one dance with you. And then you can go back to acting like I and the rest of these chumps don't exist."

After a few seconds of pondering it over, Anissa finally stood. She let him lead her back to the dance floor, but once there, she took over. If a dance was what he wanted, that was what he would get. She knew she was doing the damn thing when she felt Leon's impressive bulge against her backside as she twerked on him. The way she moved her body to the music, one might have thought her moves were choreographed. By the time the song was over and everyone began clearing out, she was still entangled in his arms. The way he stared down at her, she could tell that he didn't want their night to end like that. But unluckily for him, it had to. She stepped away from him and adjusted her shorts.

"Girl, I've been looking for your ass! It's time to go. You know these muhfuckas like to act an ass when the club lets out."

Anissa looked over her shoulder to find Brynn approaching her. She blew Leon a kiss before she was pulled out of the club. She felt like Cinderella when the clock hit midnight, except she still had both of her shoes.

Brynn was right. As soon as they made it to her G-Wagen, a group of girls started fighting, and wigs got to flying. It was a hot ghetto mess, trying to get out of that parking lot. When they finally did, Brynn told her about a new potential client she'd met, but her words seemed to mesh together. Anissa's thoughts were in another place outside of that vehicle. For some strange reason, all she could seem to think about was that last dance with Leon.

Chapter 3

For the second morning in a row, Anissa woke up to the sound of voices. However, instead of yelling and cursing, she heard the sound of laughter carry into her room. She stretched big when she sat up in her bed and checked the digital clock beside the bed. She had slept in until eleven in the morning, but that wasn't too bad for a Sunday. She was right on time for brunch. There was a spot she and Brynn went to often where they had bottomless mimosas and great food. She tossed the covers to the side and got out of bed in her short satin pajama set. In order to get out of the room, she had to step over her bags of clothes, which she'd told herself she would put away before the day was up.

Anissa left her room, and before she walked down the hallway, she peered across the hall into Brynn's room. Her eyes were met with nothing but unpacked clothing and a disheveled bed. She knew Brynn was somewhere in the condo because she would recognize the high-pitched squeal of her laugh anywhere. Anissa found her in the kitchen with a man she had never seen before.

He was wearing a navy blue suit that went well with his chocolate skin. He wasn't really a looker, but he was well groomed, and Anissa could smell the pleasant scent of his cologne from several feet away. The two of them were sitting at the island, and Brynn had some papers in front of her. They seemed to be engrossed in good conversation, and he was staring at Brynn with adoring eyes. The chemistry between them was so electric that even Anissa felt the shock waves as she approached them.

"Good morning," she said and stood on the opposite side of the island.

"Nissa!" Brynn greeted her and turned back to the man. "Bill, this is my cousin I was telling you about."

"Pleasure to meet you," Bill said to Anissa, and she saw his eyes brush over her perky breasts. "Nice to see you've joined the land of the living."

"Bill just brought over the property deed to the condo," Brynn told Anissa and motioned to the papers in front of her. "It's official. It's ours! Well, it's in my name, but you know what's mine is yours."

"Wow, that's great," Anissa said, glancing at the paperwork. "That was really nice of you, Bill."

"Whatever Desire needs, she gets," he said, smiling at Brynn. "She is and will always be very special to me."

"Baby, you never call me Desire. Stop it." Brynn rolled her eyes. "If you didn't know my legal name before, you obviously do now." She gestured to the papers again. Then she said to Anissa, "Bill's always known my legal name. He's someone who has never judged me. He sees me."

The two of them shared a look of fondness before Bill jumped up and cleared his throat. "Well, I have to leave. Debbie is waiting for me," he said, kissing Brynn's hand. "I'm wishing you two the best, and if you need anything or have any questions about the place, just give me a call."

"See you around," Brynn said, and Anissa waved her goodbye.

They watched him let himself out, and when he was gone, Brynn grinned at the papers in front of her.

"Whoever said you can't buy happiness with pussy was a damn liar. I own a fucking Benz and a condo!" She happily waved the papers in the air.

"I'm still trying to figure out how you pulled this off," Anissa commented.

"Let's just say Bill was one of my kinkier clients." Brynn grinned mischievously. "The things he likes to do in the bedroom, people might raise a questionable eye at. Not to mention we recorded a few times . . . on my phone."

"You blackmailed him?"

"I didn't have to. Like I said before, Bill is good people. But it might help that he knows I still have all that shit in my phone."

"I'm just happy we're out of that small-ass room!" Anissa said and opened the fridge. There was nothing in it but an expired gallon of milk and sandwich meat. "You want to go to brunch with me?"

"Sorry, buttercup." Brynn poked her lip out, feigning sadness. "You might have to hit Loelle's up solo today. *I* have a date. Now that we have this place, I'm tryin'a run the check up even more. I have thirty bands until my hundred stack mark when I leave this escort shit in the dust."

"I heard that. Well, I guess I will just go by myself then, since you want to be a ho."

"Oop! Don't do me. Why don't you call up that cutie you were dancing with last night? From what I could see, he was feeling you, girl. Who is he anyway?"

"Leon," Anissa answered, remembering how fine he had been. "And I didn't even get his number or give him mine."

"And why not? That muhfucka was sexy!"

"For what?" Anissa asked, and Brynn smacked her lips.

"Girl, you gotta just have fun sometimes! Date a little bit, and I don't mean turning tricks."

"You know I don't like dating for real. Not while I'm doing what I'm doing. I've seen what men do to their girls after they find out she was escorting. And the girls never live to tell the tale themselves."

"Niggas fuck all kinds of bitches for free at every hour of the day. And—"

"At least I get paid for it. I know, I know. But nah, I'd rather keep pleasure separate while I'm handling business right now."

"Make him one of your clients then. He was iced out like he has the bread to afford you," Brynn said, shrugging her shoulders like it was just that simple.

"No." Anissa shook her head. "I just don't want to."

"Wait. You *like* him, don't you?" Brynn gave her a knowing look.

"How can I like somebody I just met?" Anissa asked and tried to turn her face so Brynn wouldn't see the smile she was trying hard to hide.

"I don't know how, but I know that you do. Like him, that is."

"Stop saying that," Anissa groaned. "I don't even know the nigga."

"But you wannnnttt to," Brynn teased and then laughed when Anissa tried to hit her. "Okay, I'm about to stop fucking with you. I'm just saying, you're close to your hundred K too. You might as well start thinking ahead."

Anissa didn't say anything back because she wanted to be done with the conversation. The two of them retreated to their rooms to get ready for their days. Brynn left before Anissa but made sure to remind her what the code was to get back in the condo. Soon after, Anissa was ready to leave too. The shower she had taken refreshed her, and she got dressed in a pretty, pale pink sundress and a denim shirt tied around her waist.

Before she could walk out the door, she had to locate her cell phone, but she couldn't remember what she'd done with it when she came in the night before. Her eyes fell on the floor where the jeans shorts she had been wearing were, and she snatched them up. Sure enough, there was a bulge in one of the back pockets, and it was her phone. When she pulled it out to put in her Birkin, a small piece of paper fell out with it. Curious, she picked the paper up and looked at it to see what it was. It was a business card with LEON'S DELIGHTS on it and a phone number.

She grinned to herself, knowing that he must have slipped it into her pocket while they were dancing. She thought about what Brynn had said about hitting him up to come to brunch with her. At least five minutes passed with her just standing there looking at the number and trying to make a decision.

"Fuck it," she exhaled and dialed the number on the card. She listened to the other end of the receiver ring four times before he picked up.

"Leon speaking," his deep voice said.

"What's up? It's Anissa from last night."

"What's crazy is that I was just sitting here wondering when you were gon' find my business card in your pocket."

"I just found it." Anissa smiled into the phone. "I'm just trying to figure out when you had time to slide it in without me feeling it."

"You were bent over doing your thing," he told her. "I saw my chance, and I leaped at the opportunity. I couldn't just let you leave without taking a piece of me with you."

"Is that right?"

"Damn straight. Tell me, what you getting into today?"

"Well, that's actually why I was calling you," Anissa said and paused. She couldn't believe she was about to ask a man out on a date. That was something like a plot twist. "Are you busy right now?"

"Nah, what's up?"

"I was about to go to lunch at Loelle's. Have you heard of it?"

"Girl, what you mean have I heard of it? That's my spot. They have the best brunch in South Beach."

"Do you want to join me? In like thirty minutes?"

"Say less. I'm there."

"Cool. I'll see you soon then."

"No doubt."

They disconnected the call, and Anissa tried to tame the butterflies in her stomach. She felt like she was in high school and had finally gotten the attention of the football quarterback. It took her ten more minutes to leave the house, because she touched up her makeup and lip gloss. When she was finally satisfied with her reflection, she left the condo.

When she got to the restaurant, she parked her Audi next to a white BMW M6. After spraying herself with perfume, she opened the car door and got out.

"I bet that perfume has you smelling like a million bucks!" she heard Leon's voice say.

She glanced over at the BMW in time to see him stepping out of it. He looked ten times more handsome in the sunlight, and when he smiled, his bottom grill was almost blinding. She returned his grin and waited for him to come over to her.

"You look amazing," he said, complimenting her attire.

"You don't look so bad yourself," she said, running a hand over the shoulder of his fitted button-up. "What is this, Dior?"

"I see you know your fashion."

"A little bit. That's just one of my favorite places to shop."

"I'll keep that in mind."

The two of them made their way into the restaurant, and when they were seated, Leon seemed to not be able to keep his eyes off her. Anissa was used to being a spectacle. She was used to men ogling her outer appearance and giving her thirsty stares. But there was something different about his gaze. Something deeper. It was like he was trying to find the smallest details about her. She felt her face grow warm, and she averted her eyes to her menu.

"What are you going to have?" she asked.

"What I want isn't on the menu."

"That was corny," she said with a laugh.

"It was a little played out, wasn't it?" he said, joining her in her laugh.

"Very much so. I'm going to have the breakfast platter with bacon and, of course, a bottomless mimosa."

"I'll keep it simple and have the same thing," Leon said and called the waitress over.

He placed their order, and within minutes, the woman brought back their drinks. As Anissa slurped it down, Leon went back to staring at her.

"Do I have something on my face or something?"

"Nah. I'm just sitting here wondering if anybody has ever told you what kind of gem you are."

"Stop it," she told him, but only because at that moment the butterflies came back.

"You think I'm gaming, but I'm being dead serious. I feel like there was a reason I saw you at the club last night. I spotted you the moment you walked in with your friend."

"My cousin," she corrected him.

"Either way, you were the most beautiful woman in that bitch. Everybody wanted to get at you, but look at you now. Here with me. That's fate."

"You think so?"

"I do. You don't?"

"I don't believe in fate," she told him.

"So, what do you believe in then?"

"Money," Anissa answered bluntly. "It's the only thing that I can trust."

"You don't think you can trust me?"

"I don't know you, Leon."

"That's why I'm here now. Maybe we can get to that point." He gave her an innocent, hopeful look and reached for her hand. "I want to get to know you. Will you let me?"

"It depends on how this little date goes," she told him.

When the food came, the two of them kept talking. Soon their small talk turned into heavy conversation about anything they could think of. Anissa couldn't remember the last time she laughed so hard with somebody other than Brynn. The wall she had up hadn't been beaten completely down, but Leon had definitely chipped away at it.

When they were finished with their food, Leon paid the bill and gave her a look like he didn't want their time together to end. He reached across the table and grabbed her hands in his. "Tell me, what do you like to do?" Leon asked her.

"Didn't you already ask me that?"

"Maybe, but I don't think you answered."

"I like to shop," Anissa answered simply. "I can't seem to stay out of designer stores."

"You spend your own bag?" he asked curiously.

"Of course."

"Well, if you fuck with me the long way, you won't ever have to pull out your own wallet again."

"Is that right?"

"Damn straight. A lady of mine doesn't have to worry about ever spending her own money."

"Prove it," Anissa dared him, and Leon gave her the cutest sly smile.

"Come on. You said you like Dior, right?"

The sounds of the waves crashing into land was like music to Brynn's ears. It was such a pretty day at the beach, and the sun was beaming down on her smooth skin. The chocolate bikini she wore seemed to be painted on as she lay on her beach chair, wearing oversized sunglasses.

"If all these people weren't here watching, I would eat you up," a deep voice said, approaching her.

Brynn looked over her sunglasses at the fine hunk of meat sitting in the chair next to her. His name was Jamal, and she'd met him the night before at the club. However, unlike Anissa's little date, Jamal was a paying customer. Still, she couldn't deny the fact that he was major eye candy, and the two of them looked good together. The entire time at the beach, they'd been getting looks, probably because he looked as good in his swim trunks as she did in her bikini. She had been instantly attracted to him at the club the night before. It might have been his full beard or the fact that the waves on top of his head gave the ocean a run for its money. It was always a treat when she was physically into one of her tricks. It meant that she, hopefully, didn't have to fake it. But from the size of the print in his trunks, she wouldn't be disappointed.

"Is that for me?" Brynn asked, pointing at one of two drinks in his hand.

"It sure is," he said with a smile. "A strawberry daquiri with a double shot, just like you asked."

"You're the best, baby," she said and took the drink when he handed it to her.

She took one gulp and instantly moaned, closing her eyes. The bartender had made it just right, and not only that, but the cold liquid replenished her body in the heat. She slurped until half the drink was gone and she was on the brink of a brain freeze.

"Now what's that you were saying about eating me up?" she flirted, turning her attention back to him.

"I was just saying that I'm glad it was you I met last night. And I'm glad that it's you here with me, although it's costing me a pretty penny."

"Well worth it, baby."

"Trust me, I know. It doesn't feel like it's costing me at all," he said, taking a sip of his drink. "This isn't my first time with an escort."

"I kind of got that impression," Brynn said and eyed him down. "So, tell me something, Jamal. You're a handsome man. Tall, sexy, and educated at that. Why pay for pussy? I bet there are women all over just throwing it at you."

"You're right about that," he chuckled. "But those same women want and expect the world from me. And I can't give that yet, not with being the busy lawyer I am. Not only that, but most of them come with bedroom limits, which means I can't unleash my inner freak the way I want to. When you pay for it, the lady has to do whatever it is you like."

"And what is it you like, Jamal?"

"You'll have to wait and find out." He gave her a mischievous look. "I hope you can handle me. I usually go with one of the Delights when I need to let off my sexual steam."

"One of the Delights?" Brynn inquired curiously.

"It's an escort service with the sexiest women you'll ever meet. With as fine as you are, I thought you were one of them."

"Nope, I'm not. Sorry. How does that work, anyway? Do they have like an answering machine or account you send your payment to?"

"Nah. After the date, you pay the money to the owner, a dude well known around these parts. He doesn't play about his girls, and if you see them, you'd understand why. But you? You blow all those women out of the water."

"I bet, but I don't do the pimp thing."

"No bodyguard either?" Jamal asked and raised an eyebrow.

"Nah. I can handle myself," Brynn said and slurped down the rest of her daquiri.

"I'm sure you can," he said, and Brynn didn't notice the pitch of his voice drop. "You ready to head back to the hotel?"

"If you are, baby. This is your show. I'm just starring in it."

"I like the sound of that. Come on."

The two of them gathered up their things and left for the hotel. It was actually in walking distance since it was right on the beach. When they got inside, Brynn set her bag down and went straight for the mini fridge inside of the suite. She wanted to take another shot of something, because that daquiri was good, but she barely had a buzz.

"Tequila!" she cheered, pulling the bottle out and pouring two shots. "Here, drink with me, baby."

She handed Jamal the cup, and they downed the contents together. It burned going down, but Brynn welcomed the sensation. She went back to the fridge and poured another. After she tossed it back, she turned to face Jamal again, and a smile instantly spread across her face. Jamal was sitting on the king-sized bed facing her, only he had gotten completely naked. His thick manhood was standing at attention, and he was giving her a look that asked, "What you gonna do with it?"

As she slowly walked to him, Brynn seductively removed her bikini. When she too was naked, she rubbed all over her body, making sure to give her brown nipples extra attention. The liquor began to take effect, and the nipple stimulation was sending chills all throughout her body. He began stroking his shaft as he watched her little show.

When she got to him, she dropped to her knees and wrapped her lips around the tip of his dick and removed his hands. She worked her lips and tongue down the whole thing and didn't stop until it was knocking at the back of her throat. Once it was wet, she began giving him her two-hand bobblehead combo, the one that made the men go crazy, just like it made him. His hands gripped the edge of the bed tightly as she slobbered him down until his knees began to shake. Giving head was something that Brynn truly enjoyed doing. She could feel each one of his protruding veins on her tongue, because he was hard as a rock. After about ten minutes, she stopped sucking and worked some magic by using only her hands. With one hand, she gently rolled his soaking-wet balls, and with the other she used her thumb to massage the spot underneath the tip of his dick.

"Ahh, shit, baby. That's it. Right there! You know what you're doing, don't you?"

"You ain't seen nothing yet," Brynn told him. "Where are the condoms?"

Jamal quickly reached and pulled out a Magnum from underneath the pillow. He tore it open and rolled it down his shaft. Grabbing Brynn by the hands, he pulled her up and bent her over on the bed.

"Now it's my turn to be in control," Jamal said, positioning himself at her opening. "I've been imagining this ass bouncing back on my dick all day."

He eased his way inside of her love tunnel, but that was the gentlest he was with his monster. Once he was sure that it would all fit, he showed Brynn's little kitty cat no mercy. But it wasn't her first time being pounded out. She caught every stroke with her chest and face on the bed. She reached back and opened her cheeks so Jamal could get a better look at her glistening holes.

"Mmm," she moaned. "Do you like it, baby?"

"Hell yeah," he grunted. "I love this tight, dripping pussy."

He smacked her ass for effect and went back to digging deep inside of her wetness. Soon, she felt his thumb poking at her anus before he shoved it through and held it there. Instantly, the walls of her love tunnel clenched around his shaft, making her quiver and shout in bliss. She couldn't lie. His dick inside of her felt so good, and it wasn't long before her clit swelled up. A few strokes later, she was singing love cries in the sheets as she squirted all over them. But Jamal wasn't anywhere near done with her yet.

He flipped her over on her back and admired her body for a few moments before opening her legs and diving in face first. He slurped away at her juices the same way she'd slurped that daquiri, until her legs quaked. Her hands massaged the back of his head, cheering him on as his tongue worked magic on her clit. Every second was filled with one of her moans, and Jamal didn't stop licking until she squirted another round of juices on his face. He didn't move. He welcomed all the liquid and didn't wipe it off until she was done.

Panting, Brynn looked down to see her mess, but instead she was met with his expression. She tried to catch her breath, but he didn't let her. He gripped her legs behind her ankles and forced them back right before he slid into her again. She pinched her nipples since he hadn't given them any attention as he beat her cervix into oblivion. She could feel her last orgasm on the brink, and by the way his dick was jumping inside of her, he was close to his climax too. She opened her legs wide so that he had a good look of her pretty face and breasts. She cupped them so he could see them bouncing as he fucked her, and that was what did it. He thrust into her one more time, and she could feel him coming deep inside of her, shooting his nut into the condom. She hurried to rub away at her clit so that she could meet him at the finish line.

"Shit!" she cried as one last round of waterworks erupted between her thighs and on his pelvis.

Her back arched for a few moments until the amazing feeling subsided, and she dropped back down on the bed. Jamal held the condom as he pulled out of her, careful not to leak anything inside of her. After she finally caught her breath, she stood up and snatched her bikini off the ground. Jamal collapsed on the bed, and she went to the bathroom with her beach bag to clean up. She had a dress and some sandals inside of it. She usually didn't bother with underwear. She used a towel and some soap to take a vigorous "ho" bath until she was satisfied. Afterward, when she was dry and dressed with her bag on her shoulder, she left the bathroom to collect her money.

Jamal used that time to get dressed as well. He was wearing a pair of shorts and a black T-shirt. She gave him a big smile that he didn't return, but she figured he was just worn out. She pointed at the nightstand beside the bed.

"Is the money in there?" she asked, but Jamal just looked at her. "Hello, earth to Jamal. I know it was that good, but don't be mesmerized, baby. There is plenty more where that came from."

"You know, Desire, you should really get a pimp," Jamal told her.

"Okayyy, noted. What does that have to do with my money though?"

"You ain't getting no money," he told her bluntly, and Brynn was completely blindsided.

"What do you mean, I'm not getting my money? You owe me five bands, so pay up," she snapped.

"Bitch, I'm not paying you shit!" he said meanly. Gone was the gentleman he'd been all day. "Maybe if you had someone to force me to pay up, you'd have your money. Now you need to get out of my room."

"Not until you give me my money," Brynn said, getting in his face. "You don't get to fuck for free."

"Well, I just did."

"Hell nah. You're gonna pay me." Brynn tried to dig in his pockets, but Jamal backhanded her hard in the face.

The blow knocked her back, and she could taste blood in her mouth due to a busted lip. The anger welled up in her like too much helium in a balloon, and she was about to burst. It had been a while since she'd dealt with a client willing to get physical with her, and Jamal was about to learn the hard way why she didn't need a pimp.

Jamal went to try to force her out of the hotel room, but by then Brynn had already pulled her pistol out of the beach bag. In one quick motion, she pistol-whipped him hard in the nose, and it instantly started leaking. She hit him again and again before cocking it and aiming it at his face. He fell to his knees and put his hands up in the air.

"Like I said, muhfucka, where the *fuck* is my money?" she asked again.

"I'm gonna call the police and tell them you robbed me," he threatened.

"And I'm gonna tell them you raped me and I had to defend myself. Who do you think they'll believe?" Brynn pressed the pistol against his forehead. "Either that or they can just find your body with the dick blown off. And I'll be sure to do that part *before* I kill you."

"H . . . here," he rushed, suddenly having a change of heart. He hurried to pull out his wallet and hand her a big wad of cash. "It's all there. I swear."

"It better be, or I'll find you," Brynn promised.

She eyeballed the cash and stuffed it in her bag before backing up to the exit. She didn't stop pointing the gun until she was at the room door and had to put it away. Once out of the room, she hurried out of the hotel, not knowing if Jamal was going to try to come after her.

She was fuming when she got to her vehicle at what he had tried to pull, but then she realized that she had nobody to blame but herself. She had been too lippy at the beach. Not only that, but the shots of tequila had made her forget her number one rule: always collect the money first.

As she drove off, she looked at her face and groaned. Her busted lip had swollen, and it was going to take some days for it to heal. That meant she would have to cancel her dates, and *that* meant she would have to miss out on money. She wanted to turn and go back to the hotel so she could actually put two bullets in Jamal's head, but she didn't. She definitely wouldn't be able to make any money if she was in jail. So instead she just went to the condo so she forget about Jamal trying to play her.

Brynn put the code in to unlock the door, expecting to have the condo to herself for a few hours, but to her surprise Anissa was sitting in the kitchen. That would have been fine if she were alone. Sitting next to her was the same guy she had been dancing with at the club the night before, and by their feet was a plethora of shopping bags.

"Umm, what's going on?" she asked with a raised eyebrow. "Why is he here?"

"Oh, hey, Brynn," Anissa said with a dopey smile on her face. "This is Leon."

"Okay, hi, Leon," Brynn said, not taking her eyes off Anissa. "Nissa, we just got here, and you're already letting niggas up in the spot?"

"Cuz, chill. He's cool," Anissa said, taking note of Brynn's pissed-off expression.

"Cool? You don't know him from a can of paint. I said date him, not let him know where we lay our heads. I don't care how much Dior he bought you. Baby, you gotta bounce."

That time she looked at Leon, and she had her thumb pointed at the door when she did.

"My bad. I ain't mean no disrespect," Leon said, getting up from the stool. He turned to Anissa and kissed her on the cheek. "Hit me. You know I'ma come running anytime you call."

When he was gone, Anissa smacked her lips and looked at Brynn like she was crazy. "Yo, man. Why you tripping so hard?"

"Because you don't just let niggas up in our spot like that! You don't know him, stupid! We got all our bread in here, Nissa. Come *on*. Use your head!"

"Leon ain't tryin'a steal nothing from me! Maybe you aren't mad at me, but at whoever did that to your lip!" Anissa jumped up and stormed to her room.

Brynn felt like a mother who had just had to chastise her kid. Although she knew she had a reason to be mad, she knew Anissa was right. She walked in mad. Seeing them had just been the icing on the cake. She sighed and went back to Anissa's room. The door was open, and when she peeked in, Anissa was sitting on the bed scrolling through her phone.

"Look, I'm sorry, all right?" she said from the doorway. "My date today tried not to pay me. He said he was used to booking dates through some escort service here. Delights or something."

"Delights?" Anissa asked, finally glancing up from her phone. She had an indifferent look on her face.

"Yeah. He said that's where he usually gets his girls from. And since they have a pimp to make him pay and I don't, he thought he didn't have to pay me. Shit got ugly shortly after that."

"What?" Anissa asked. "Are you good?"

"Yeah. I look better than him right now anyway. And I got my money, without a pimp. I would never have one, ever. They take all of your money and try to kill you when you don't want to fuck for them anymore. Plus, I'm almost out of this game." Brynn shrugged. "Anyways, I didn't have to treat you like a kid, but you have to respect this spot. I don't want any niggas up in here. This is our sanctuary. Not to mention all my shit is in here, and I don't know that nigga."

"You're right, and I'm sorry too," Anissa sighed. "I guess I got a little carried away. He just showed me a really good time, and I lost myself for a minute. But you don't have to worry about that again."

"Okay, cool. I love you. I'm about to go get some ice for my lip. I'll be in my room if you need me." Brynn took a step back from the door.

"Hey, Brynn?"

"Yeah?"

"Did your date tell you the name of the pimp he pays, by chance?"

"No, why?"

"No reason."

Chapter 4

A week had passed since Anissa had seen Leon, and he had been blowing her phone up. And that night wasn't any different. She lay in bed staring at a show playing on her new fifty-inch television mounted on the wall. The simple truth was that she had just been so busy going on dates and making money that she didn't have time to hang out with him.

The complicated truth was in between her fingers at that very moment.

It was the business card Leon had given her, the one that said LEON'S DELIGHTS. She wished she'd gone into more detail about what he did for a living, but she didn't want him asking her the same questions. So, she had played it safe the day they spent together. However, now she was wondering what exactly his occupation was. He spent a good $3,000 on her without blinking while shopping. He wanted to go to a few more stores for her, but she was the one who was ready to call it a day. That night he'd called her once already, and when her phone rang again, she looked down and saw it was him.

She sighed. "Hello?"

"Finally you decide to answer. I've been missing that voice."

"What's going on, Leon?" she asked.

"Nothing, just wondering why you've been avoiding me."

"I've been busy working."

"What is it that you do again?"

"I'm a businesswoman," Anissa answered, not missing a beat, and before he could ask her to go into detail, she spoke again. "What have you been up to?"

"Wondering when I can take you out again. Are you busy tonight?"

"A little," Anissa said and glanced at the show she'd barely been watching.

"Can you come somewhere with me?"

"Ummm . . ."

"Please? I just really want to see you," he begged, and she smiled. He sounded so pitiful that it was adorable.

"All right, crybaby. Where?"

"It's a surprise. Can I come pick you up in forty? I'm finishing up here, and then I can be there."

"Yes. That's enough time for me to get ready. How should I dress?"

"However you want. Your girl isn't gon' shoot me when I pull up, is she?"

"No," Anissa laughed. "Just call me when you get here, and I'll come outside."

"All right. See you soon, queen."

When they disconnected, Anissa felt tingles all over her body. She had to admit that she was excited to see him. She hopped up and rummaged through the clothes hanging in her walk-in closet before settling on a pair of jeans and a cute off-the-shoulder bodysuit. On her feet she decided to rock the pair of Dior sneakers Leon had bought her.

By the time she had put some fresh curls in her wig and glossed her lips, he was calling to say he was outside. Brynn was gone on a date already, so that was the main reason Leon didn't have anything to worry about. She grabbed her purse and was out the door in minutes. That time Leon pulled up, he was in a red Mustang, and when he saw her come through the front doors of the building, he smiled big.

"Damn, you look better every time I see you," he said out the window. "Come on, get in."

He leaned and pushed open the passenger door for her. As soon as she got in, she smelled the Black Ice car freshener hanging from his rearview mirror. She smiled because it was the same scent she had in her own car. She admired his vehicle. She wasn't really a Ford fan, but she had to admit the newer-model Mustang was nice.

"You be renting cars or something?" she asked, and he made a face.

"I'm insulted. I don't rent. I buy everything. Ain't a point in having shit if you don't own it."

"Okay, okay. My bad. So where are we going?"

"It's a surprise, queen," he said mischievously. "Just know I have a nice surprise for you."

"And what's that?"

"You'll see."

"Whatever. What kind of music you listening to? Probably some hood shit," Anissa said and turned the volume in the car up. Surprisingly, no loud bass came. In fact, the soft crooning of Lauryn Hill filled the vehicle, and she gave him a shocked look. "You like Lauryn?"

"Of course. Who don't like Lauryn? This is the kind of music that speaks to the soul."

"What do you know about talking to the soul?"

"Probably a little more than you, Miss Don't Let Nobody Close to Me."

"There's a reason I'm like that."

"And what's that reason? You don't think you deserve love or something, shawty?"

"It's personal. I'm just not somebody anyone should love right now."

"How do you know unless you give someone a chance?"

"It's just complicated, okay?" Anissa turned her head and looked out the window.

They didn't say anything else until Leon turned into the parking lot of a dance studio. It was in a plaza with other businesses, and she was confused because the lights in the studio were off. She looked at Leon, who was already staring at her with a smile on his face.

"Are we going in there?" she asked, wrinkling her forehead.

"Yes."

"But I don't have dancing shoes." She pointed to her sneakers.

"That's why I stopped and grabbed these earlier today. I remembered your size from the other day," he told her, pulling a shoebox from the back seat and handing it to her. Inside was a pair of black open-toe heels. "I was hoping you'd come out with me tonight."

"Why didn't you just tell me to wear something with heels?" she asked.

"Because I wanted you to wear what you wanted," he said with a shoulder shrug.

"You're sweet. Well, you're lucky I put some lotion on my feet," she said and changed into the heels.

When she was done, Leon got out and went around to open her door. He helped her out of the car and held her hand all the way until they got to the front door of the dance studio. He held it open for her to walk through, and then he followed. She almost gasped at the sight, and her hands flew to her chest.

The lights inside weren't off. They had just been turned down. Leon had set the place up to mirror a small high school prom. There were strobe lights and beautiful silver decorations hanging from the ceiling. He even had a tall black balloon arch with a wall of silver streamers behind it for them to take pictures under. To the side there was a table filled with food and a punch bowl. A table set for two was in the middle of the dance floor, and Leon led her to it. There was a remote on the table, and he pressed a button on it for music to start playing.

"Leon, this is . . . Nobody has ever done anything like this for me before," she said when they were seated across from each other. "This is—"

"Too much?"

"Perfect," she finished.

"I'm just glad you agreed to come, because all this would have gone to waste if you didn't."

"What would make you do something like this, Leon?"

"I knew from the night I met you that you were different. So, I knew in order to get you to take me seriously, I had to *do* different. And plus, there is something about seeing you smile."

If Anissa were a little lighter, she was sure Leon would have witnessed her blush. She wanted to fight off the feelings coming over her for Leon, but she couldn't. Not only was he fine in his silk black collared shirt, but he was kind to her just because. Jagged Edge began playing, and she reached her hands out to him.

"Will you dance with me?"

"I'm supposed to ask you that," Leon said and pretended to clear his throat. "Anissa, can I have this dance?"

"You're so silly," she giggled as they got up.

"What? Ain't that how them boys used to do it in high school?"

"I guess, but I know for sure none of them looked as good as you."

They moved close to each other, and she wrapped her arms around his neck while he placed his on the small of her back. It had been a while since she slow danced. It was so intimate, just staring up into his eyes and letting the music take control of their bodies. Although their bodies were pressed against each other, Anissa wanted to be even closer to him, so she rested her head on his shoulder. The rhythm of his heart was better than any tune Jagged Edge could sing. They swayed their bodies through two more songs before going to take pictures and getting some finger foods.

It was the sweetest date Anissa had ever been on, but still there was something weighing on her mind. She couldn't let herself fall for him without knowing the truth. When they were back seated at the table, she watched him take a bite of his sandwich. She was waiting for the right time to bring it up, but then she realized there was no right time.

"Leon?"

"What's up, queen?"

"Can I ask you something?"

"Anything."

"What is it that you do for work?" When she asked, she saw him briefly pause in his chewing. "I mean, you gave me a card the other day that said 'Leon's Delights.' What is that, exactly?"

He didn't say anything for a few moments. In fact, he went on eating his food as if Anissa hadn't just asked him a question. When finally he was done, he stood up and held his hand out.

"Come on. I can show you exactly what Leon's Delights is."

There were some woman who turned their noses up at women who used what they had to get what they wanted, but not Brynn. Especially since she was such a woman. She'd learned the power of pussy at the ripe age of 18 thanks to her high school English teacher, Mr. Hank. All it took for him to change her failing grade to passing was a pair of her worn panties and a few photos. After that, it was a wrap. She learned how to get into men's heads using the allure of what was between her legs. Although there may have been some men who could resist her charm, she hadn't met one of them yet, mainly because the thing that set her apart from other girls in the game was that she still believed in being good to people. While, yes, clients were paying to be pleased sexually, they were also paying to be *seen*. And Brynn made sure she saw them. She also listened to them, and she offered them counsel when she could. To her it was easy money because she was simply just being herself.

The sound of someone clearing their throat pulled Brynn from the clutches of her own mind. She was so lost thinking about how easy men were that she had forgotten she was on a dinner date with Jason, one of her wealthiest clients. He was a brown-skinned man in his mid-forties. His head was shaven completely bald, but if anything, it made him look sexier, especially since he took care of his body. He had made a lot of his money investing in products, and he also owned many properties around Florida. Brynn met him before Anissa had come to stay with her. She'd been dreaming back then, scouting the perfect venue for her salon. But she wasn't dreaming anymore.

"Care to tell me what you find so amusing?" he asked, staring at the smile frozen on her face.

"No, I don't. You wouldn't find it funny," she said with a small giggle.

"Oh. I thought you were going to say something about how this salmon is better than the last time we came to Dru's," he said with a hearty laugh, wiping his mouth with a napkin. "I'm glad you talked me into giving this place another chance."

"You know you can always trust my intuition, baby," she said and watched him down his fourth glass of wine.

She glanced down at her plate and saw that she had barely touched her food, not because she wasn't hungry, but because she'd been spending the entire dinner trying to find an opening to talk about what she really wanted to talk about. Seeing that there wasn't really a perfect time, she decided that maybe she should just wait until he finished the bottle of wine he'd purchased by himself.

"Jason baby?"

"Yes, my Desire."

"Can I talk to you about something?"

"As long as it's not anything about my wife, always, baby," Jason said and sat up a little straighter.

Jason had always made it clear to Brynn that he had no intention of leaving his wife ever for anybody. That had always been fine with Brynn. She never got too attached. It went without saying that she felt the two of them had formed a nice bond since they'd met. Bill might have been her first client, but Jason was her favorite. For him to be almost twice her age, he was able to keep up with her in and out of the bedroom. He was the first man to ever take her out of the country. They went to Thailand and rode elephants. Brynn's Instagram story was popping that weekend. It was amazing. Brynn never asked why he couldn't do the things he did with her with his wife. She figured Jason was just an older man looking for some young fun.

"Have I ever brought up your wife? You've made it quite clear that the topic is off-limits," Brynn told him. "What I want to talk about is that property a few miles from South Beach that you have for sale. The one that used to be a pet grooming place."

"What about it?"

"I just wanted to know if anyone has anybody put in an offer on it."

"Not yet, but I have a few potential buyers coming to look at it by the end of the week. What's it to you, Madame Desire? Are you looking into getting a property?"

"Not just any property. That property. For my salon. Do you remember the one I told you about?"

"I do," Jason said and rubbed his fingers along his thick, graying mustache. "When we first met."

"I have my cosmetology license already and some startup money. I just need a location. And that property would be perfect. I'm ready to start the next phase of my life. I'm ready to make an honest living."

"And what, leave all this behind?" Jason motioned around the divine restaurant with one hand. "That's a two-thousand-dollar dress you're wearing. I know because I bought it. I don't look at you any differently because I have to pay for your time. You are still one of the loveliest ladies I've ever met."

"Thank you, baby. I enjoy spending time with you, Jason," Brynn said. "I do. It's just that no girl plans on spending her life doing this kind of work forever. There was always an expiration on this."

"Some girls don't have that luxury." Jason gave her a curious look and paused for a few moments. He called their server back to their table and ordered another bottle of their finest wine. When he turned back to Brynn, he said, "If you want the building, you can have it."

"No." Brynn shook her head. It was like a light bulb had gone off in her head. She'd been prepared to talk Jason down on the price, not accept it as a gift. She thought back to Bill and how he'd just handed over the condo to her, no questions asked. It was a blessing, but still, she didn't want any more handouts. "I'm tired of people just giving me things. I have money. I've been saving to start my business. I want to own it."

"So, you have two hundred thousand dollars to give to me right now? Because if so, I'll take it," Jason said with a hearty chuckle.

"No, I don't," Brynn said with a sigh. "But I can give you fifty thousand and pay you monthly until the building is paid off."

"Desire," Jason said, reaching across the table to hold her hands in his, "I am going to be quite honest with you because you have been nothing but respectful of me during the time we've spent together. My wife and I—"

"You don't have to explain anything to me, Jason."

"It's important," he said, staring deeply into her eyes. "My wife and I have been very much in love with each other for the past fifteen years. I tell you never to ask about her because I don't want to talk about her. It hurts too much."

"What hurts?"

"Dalia was in a car accident last year that has left her brain-dead. She has been on life support ever since. That was the hardest time in my life, knowing I would never be able to have her as I once had her. It was too much to bear, and I was too much of a coward to pull the plug. But then I met you, by chance. And you reminded me so much of her, of us. You even have a beauty mark above your lip like she does. It was crazy and I was selfish. I wanted to have you in my life, no matter the cost, as I've proven time and time again. And I would pay that price all over again because you, Desire, turned the most trying time of my life into something beautiful. You made me feel alive again, and through you, I've found the strength to finally move on with my life."

"You're . . . you're gonna pull the plug on your wife because of me?" Brynn asked barely above a whisper.

"No, not because of you." He shook his head, calming the alarmed expression on her face. "Because it's time to.

The only reason I kept her on life support for so long was because I couldn't bear to be in a world without her. But now I realize that she's already gone. I'm just keeping her body in pain. Thank you for helping me realize that."

"But I don't do anything but come places with you sometimes," Brynn said, still not understanding. "And you paid me to do that."

"You might be right about that, but one thing money can't buy is genuine kindness," Jason said with a smile. "And you've shown me that. In truth, I don't feel like I've paid you what you're worth. So, take the property and open your salon. Shit, open a hundred of them. I'll have my assistant draw up the paperwork and get it to you by the end of the week. Accept it as payment for tonight. Our last date."

By then the server had brought back the bottle of wine and refilled their glasses. Jason held his up and waited for Brynn to do so too. It took her a moment, but with a slightly shaky hand she held hers up and hit it against his glass. She couldn't believe her luck.

"Cheers," he said.

"Cheers," Brynn said with a smile.

Chapter 5

"A pimp!"

"Huh?" Brynn asked, stirring, only half awake.

Anissa had barged into her room first thing the next morning and jumped on her cousin's bed. She hadn't gotten any sleep the night before after she'd gotten home from her date with Leon, and there was good reason. Brynn tried to pull the covers back over her head, but Anissa snatched them back down.

"Wake up!"

"Okay, okay! I'm up! What's so important that you had to come wake me up at—" Brynn stopped talking to glance at her cell phone for the time. "Bitch it's eight o-clock in the damn morning! This better be good!"

"He's a pimp!"

"What? Who's a pimp?"

"Leon!"

"Leon? How do you know?"

"I went out with him last night, and . . . Girl, let me just tell you what happened . . ."

"Welcome to my humble abode, shawty." Leon grinned and held his arms out wide.

He and Anissa stood in the foyer of the biggest house she had ever been in. She was blown away. She should have known by the fact that there was a guest house that the inside of the main house would be extravagant. There was a large crystal chandelier hanging above them, and she glanced around at the areas of the house she could see. *The furniture in the living room looked as if it had never been sat on.*

"Wow, Leon. This place is amazing."

"Thank you. I tried to do a little something with it."

"It's more than a little something."

She loved the stained wooden floors and the circular staircase because they gave the house a modern look. The living room had sexy red leather couches and silver decor hanging from the walls. Anissa couldn't see the kitchen from where she stood, but she knew it had to be nice. She wanted to explore, but first she had to know one thing.

"How?" she asked, furrowing her brow at him.

"How can I afford this?"

"This and the cars. Are you some type of ball player or something?"

Leon laughed. "Nah, I wish. This is the house my dad left me."

"Well, was he a ball player?"

"Believe it or not, I come from a family of farmers. My dad and his brothers own a lot of land and a farm in Texas. A whole bunch of grocery stores shop with that farm and spend a lot of paper. When my pops died, his portion of that money started coming to me."

"So, you're set for life then, pretty much."

"If my uncles don't have a say in my cash flow. They feel that since I ain't worked hands-on in the business since college, I don't deserve the perks. Just in case they ever get a good case to take to a judge, I keep a few side hustles."

"Like Leon's Delights?"

"That's right," Leon said, crossing his arms and leaning on a wall.

"I thought you were going to tell me exactly what Leon's Delights is," Anissa said, taking note of the smirk on his face.

"Daddy, is that you?" a voice called down the stairs.

Shocked, Anissa's eyes widened as she whisked her head back and forth from Leon to the place where she'd heard the voice. The voice had called him "daddy," but it didn't sound like it belonged to a child. It sounded like a grown woman, and Anissa's suspicions were proven right when the woman walked down the stairs. She was Anissa's height and thick in all the right places, but she had a small tummy poking out from under the shirt of her pajamas, which, by the way, were way too sexy for Leon to say she was a friend. When she saw Leon, she smiled big.

"Daddy, I thought I heard you. I missed you! Wait, who is she?"

"Um, excuse me," Anissa scoffed and pointed her thumb toward the newcomer. "What's going on here?"

"That's CoCo. You didn't think I lived in this big house all alone, did you?"

"Um, yes. Because you never mentioned you had a girl. I thought you were single."

"I am single."

"Then why do you have a half-naked bitch standing on your staircase?"

"Um, daddy, who is the new girl calling a bitch?" CoCo asked, rolling her neck.

"CoCo, baby, why don't you go get the others and come on back here, okay?" Leon suggested.

"New girl?" Anissa whispered to herself, making a face. She was nothing short of confused as she tried to make sense of everything that was taking place. She was dreaming, she had to have been. Anissa pinched herself on the arm, but the pain let her know that she was very much awake. When she glanced back up, CoCo was back, but she wasn't alone. She had two other girls with her, both very pretty and wearing similar revealing pajamas.

"*Leon, what's going on here?*" *Anissa asked, turning to him.*

"*Queen, I'd like to introduce you to some very important people in my life. You've already met CoCo. Standing next to her with the light skin and long, curly hair is Angel. And don't she just look angelic? And that there next to her, looking like a Hershey's Kiss, is Harmony. These are Leon's Delights, the best you'll find far and wide.*"

Anissa listened to him talk and tried to pinpoint why his words sounded so familiar. No, not his words. It was how he was talking. It was like something from a movie.

"*Leon? Why do you sound like a pimp?*" *Anissa asked and took a step back.*

He turned to her and smiled big, flashing his grill. She was hoping that he would put her thoughts at ease, but everything added up to one thing.

"*Ooh, daddy doesn't like being called a pimp,*" *CoCo said, sticking her lips out like Anissa was about to get in trouble.*

"*She's right. I don't like the word 'pimp,' queen. I prefer the term 'woman connoisseur.'*"

"*Nah, nigga, you're a pimp,*" *Anissa said, disgusted.* "*Is that why you've been so nice to me? Why you wouldn't let up? Nigga, are you trying to recruit me?*"

"*I just thought you had some flame to you, that's all, shawty,*" *Leon said with a shrug.* "*Had me pulling out all the stops just to get your attention. I spent three bands on you just because. Imagine how much more money there is where that came from. I mean, it ain't no secret what you do for a living. Any guy with eyes can see that you use that little pussy to make all your paper.*"

"*Fuck you, Leon,*" *Anissa spat and tried to leave, but he grabbed her by the arm.*

"*Listen, Anissa. I have a lot of high-end clients who would pay double just to get next to a girl like you, no cap. You got something special about you, and I'm just tryin'a get some money with you. I mean, you like how I've treated you so far, right?*"

For a moment Anissa was stuck. Her mouth was even frozen slightly open. So many thoughts were going through her head, but they all had the same result: her slapping the hell out of him for even having the audacity to come at her like that. Everything had been a hoax, and she had almost fallen for it. She'd heard how smooth pimps were, but it was the first time she'd ever experienced one in person. Leon had to be the smoothest one.

"*You almost had me,*" *she told him when the spell was broken.* "*The only reason I ever even gave you the time of day was because I thought maybe you really liked me. But I would never split my money with a pimp. Get the fuck out my way before I shoot your ass.*"

She snatched her arm away from him and yanked open the heavy front door. When she left, she didn't look back. Her Uber couldn't come fast enough because all she wanted to do was go home.

"Please tell me at least part of that story was fiction," Brynn said when Anissa was through talking. She had sat up and was gripping her covers as she listened to Anissa's crazy story. When Anissa shook her head, letting her know it was all fact, Brynn let the covers go and balled her hands into fists. Anissa had forgotten about her cousin's mean streak and was partially regretting telling her the story now, mainly because Brynn was really the type to pull up to Leon's house and give him a piece of her mind.

"That dirty muthafucka!" she exclaimed and hit the bed. "Are you okay? What's his address? I got something for his ass."

"Cuz, calm down!"

"My bad. I just can't believe he really tried to play you like that."

"Girl, he rented out a whole dance studio. I thought he was one of the good ones. But if it seems too good to be true—"

"It probably is!" Brynn finished and shook her head. "Well, I'm glad his ass is out of the picture then. I'm sorry your night ended up being so trashy, but I have some good news."

"What?"

"Guess."

"Brynn, you know I hate guessing," Anissa said, giving her a serious face.

"I know, plus you probably wouldn't get this right anyway. But I got a venue for the salon!"

"Wait, what?" Anissa squealed excitedly. "Like, for real? What happened to 'wait until we reach the goal'?"

"Well, let's just say I got a pretty good deal on this place," Brynn told her with a happy grin. "Oh, my God, Nissa, it's so *perfect,* too. It's not too far from South Beach, which means the area is going to be flooded with people constantly, and that's not all."

"What?" Anissa asked, and Brynn grabbed her hands.

"It's big enough for both my salon and your boutique. We can get a wall put up with a door that leads from one to the other. We can call it something like She Sassy. What do you say? Will you go into business with me? Fuck this escort shit. Fuck everything I said before. We can do it now. We *should* do it now."

Life had been coming at Anissa faster than it ever had in her whole existence. It was like every time one thing happened, she barely had time to process it before something else was hurling full speed her way. At least that time it was good news.

She looked into Brynn's face and saw that she was dead serious, so serious that she had tears in the corners of her eyes. Anissa enjoyed the power that escorting gave her over men, but being a business owner would mean ten times more. There was only one correct answer to Brynn's proposition.

"Yes."

"Yes?"

"Yes!" Anissa exclaimed, and the two embraced and fell sideways on the bed in a fit of laughter. "We're going to be business owners! But one thing, bitch."

"What?" Brynn asked when they let each other go and were lying on their backs.

"We are *not* calling it She Sassy!"

Chapter 6

Starting a business was way more work that what either Anissa or Brynn anticipated. In their minds, they envisioned the finished result only, not the hours of hard work and labor they would have to put in. They were fortunate enough that the prior business had done all the major work to the building. All Brynn had to order were her chairs, sinks, everything she needed to do hair, and decor. She planned on having other hairdressers rent booths from her so they could do hair out of her shop.

Anissa, on the other hand, had to be a little craftier with her boutique. She hired an interior decorator to come in and have their way with her side of the building. By the time she was done, Anissa knew she was worth every dime spent. All the shelves and racks that held clothes and shoes were made of glass. The chairs and ottomans on the main floor and inside the dressing room were pink with gold trim. The gold on the chairs matched the golden light fixtures hanging from the ceiling. Once Anissa got in cahoots with the perfect clothing vendors, she was in the game.

It felt like she was in a dream whenever she walked around her store and passed the beautiful pieces hanging on the walls or saw the cute shoes waiting to be bought. She and Brynn had agreed to call the entire building "Groove," because whether it was your hair or your outfit, you wanted to look the part to get your groove on.

After two and a half long months of working day in and day out and getting all the legalities out of the way, the evening of Groove's grand opening had finally come. It was the middle of September, and Anissa couldn't have thought of a better way to end the summer. However, she was nervous. She knew because as she stood in her bedroom getting ready in the mirror, she was struggling to put on her favorite diamond necklace. Not only were her fingers a little shaky, they were moist due to her anxiety.

"Oh, my God!" she groaned, just about sick of the thing.

"Here, girl, let me help you. Can't have you launching that expensive-ass necklace out the window."

Brynn had entered the room just in time to see Anissa struggling with the clasp of the necklace. She looked elegant in her floor-length, off-the-shoulder magenta gown. Her makeup was done flawlessly, and her lips matched the color of the dress. She wore her hair up with a swoop in the front that was secured by a diamond pin. She looked like a princess.

"Thank you," Anissa sighed gratefully and let Brynn take over.

She smoothed her blush-colored dress down on her hips and gave herself a once-over. Her mermaid silhouette dress was sleeveless with a deep V neckline and glitter detail. The diamond necklace, now firmly around her neck, was the icing on the cake. She smiled at her reflection and tucked one of her rod curls behind her ear.

"You did a good job on your makeup tonight. I'm loving the natural glam," Brynn admired.

"Thank you, Princess Brynn. You look like royalty," Anissa said, shooting compliments right back.

"Oh, my goodness," Brynn sighed and stepped to the side so they could both be seen in Anissa's full-length mirror. "Can you believe that not too long ago we were sharing a small-ass room?"

"Now look at us. Business owners!"

"Now aren't you glad you saved all of the money you made from your dates?" Brynn teased.

"Hell yeah," Anissa admitted. "Because this whole process would have taken longer if we didn't have the cash already on hand to make it happen. Do you think there will be a lot of people there tonight?"

"I'm sure there will be. Shit, there better be with all of the promo I paid for!" Brynn said with raised brows. "I put flyers everywhere and even got us an ad on The Shaderoom and Baller Alert. Plus, I have two stylists who will be working tonight for back to school."

"Okay, now I'm even more nervous. Are you sure I look okay?"

"Yes!" Brynn exclaimed. "You look like a lady. Now come on, we have to get going. I can't wait until all the hating-ass bitches back in the A see us cut the ribbon to our business! Ahhh!"

On the way there, Anissa's nerves calmed down. They'd taken a few celebratory shots before leaving the condo, and she was feeling good about that night. She knew her mother, Diana, wouldn't have been proud of her selling her body to make money, but look at what it had done. It had given her something *to* be proud of, and for that she would never have any regrets.

"Oh, shit," Brynn said as they rounded the corner and drove past the business.

"Whoa," Anissa commented when she saw how many people were standing outside of Groove. "They're around the block, girl! This is crazy!"

"I know. Let me hurry up and park this car, because I need to be seen in this dress, okay?"

Brynn turned another corner so she could pull and park behind the building where their team was waiting for them. Brynn had hired two talented hairstylists,

Tamar and Ru. Tamar was a short woman who rocked her hair in a natural pixie cut. She was a little loud, but she meant no harm. Plus, she could braid the hell out of some hair. Ru was everyone's favorite transsexual. She might not have been born a woman, but baby had more class than a school. She liked wearing different-colored lace wigs every day, slayed makeup, and stayed up on all the fashion.

Anissa hired two employees as well, Gia and Alexus. Gia was heavier set, but she could dress, and that was what sold Anissa on her. She had made it a point to order plus sizes into the store and knew that by Gia not only working there but wearing the clothes, it would make more voluptuous woman unafraid to shop at Groove. Alexus, on the other hand, was skinny, but she had curves where it mattered. She was a pretty Hispanic girl, and Anissa could tell that she was a firecracker. That was okay with her because that meant Alexus wouldn't take any mess from anyone. They were all dressed, refined, and in the middle of taking shots of Patrón when they saw their bosses.

"And the ladies of the hour have arrived!" Ru said, lifting her plastic shot cup in the air. Her voice was high-pitched, and she had the biggest smile on her face. She was so pretty, and her cheekbones were praiseworthy. She grabbed two more shot cups and filled them to the rim.

"Yup, g'on 'head and give them shots to them girls!" Tamar said loudly. "Y'all doing something that black girls all over the world dream of! I'm so proud to be part of it!"

"Thank you." Anissa grinned and took one of the cups. "But none of this would be possible if it weren't for Brynn."

"Save the speech for when we get up in there. Don't babysit the shot. Throw that shit back!" Brynn teased as she too took a cup.

The six of them held their shots up before tossing the alcohol to the back of their throats. Ru took the empty cups and threw them in the dumpster before they all made their way to the red carpet in front of the building. The moment that Brynn and Anissa were spotted, cheers in the crowd erupted and flashes went off. Anissa couldn't lie, she felt like a star. There were two red bows, one in front of Brynn's door and the other in front of Anissa's. Before they were handed scissors to cut them, Tamar gave Brynn a microphone.

"I just want to thank everyone for taking time out of their evenings to come out and support Groove!" she said with her hand over her chest. "Opening up a salon where I could provide opportunities to other women just like me has always been a dream of mine. I'm even more grateful to have my cousin not only right beside me, but right next door to me with her own boutique. I know you all are going to love Groove, and we plan on being around for a long time. This moment is so surreal to me, and I'm so appreciative to all of you for showing love tonight!"

The crowd erupted into even more cheers when Brynn swapped the microphone for a pair of big scissors. Anissa was given a pair just as big, and she positioned them to cut her bow. She and Brynn looked at each other, flashing all of their teeth, before they started counting in unison.

"One, two, three!"

On "three" they cut their ribbons and screamed loudly with the crowd. Groove was officially open for business. The evening continued with music, food, and for Anissa, a lot of sales. She couldn't say she was shocked at how fast things were flying off the racks and shelves, but she could say that she felt bad for Gia and Alexus. They were running around like chickens with their heads chopped off while Anissa rang items up. Even though it was busy, she was all smiles, because knowing all the money she was making made her happy. It wasn't until she heard a familiar voice that the smile dropped.

"Excuse me, do you have this in a size small?"

Anissa looked up from the register and right into Leon's eyes. He had an innocent look on his face as if he weren't doing anything wrong. In his hands was a cute pink lingerie teddy with feathers on the bosom.

"Mmm, mm, mm. Still as beautiful as I remember," Leon said, eyeing her down in her dress.

She had to admit that he was looking good too in his Dior fitted T-shirt and jeans. However, it was his insides that made him ugly. The attraction that she had once felt for him was long gone. He'd tried calling her a few times, but she never answered. She had nothing to say to him and for sure didn't have any interest in seeing him.

"What are you doing here, Leon?" she asked.

"I heard through the grapevine that you were opening up a store. I wanted to come check you out, see what all the hype was about, you know, maybe pick some shit up for my girls."

"All right, one of the girls on the floor can help you with that."

"Damn, that's how it is? I'm tryin'a spend some money in your store, and you just gon' brush me off like that?" Leon asked, and Anissa turned her lip up.

"I mean, you don't have to spend your money in here. Matter of fact . . ." Anissa held up a finger as if to tell him to wait. She reached under the register, grabbed a metal lock box, and opened it. There was nothing but cash and a small handgun inside. After quickly counting out $3,000, she handed it to him.

"What's this for, shawty?" he asked, looking at the money in his hand.

"That's the money you spent on me when you took me shopping. I don't want you to ever feel like I owe you *anything,*" she said with a hand on her hip. "Now if you'll excuse me, I have customers to tend to. Like I said, one of the girls on the floor can help you with that teddy."

"A'ight, I'm picking up what you're putting down, baby girl," he said with a cunning smile. "Just know that if this doesn't work out, you always have a job with me."

"And I'm letting you know that that will never happen," Anissa told him, looking square in his eyes.

He gave a small laugh and turned away from the register. She watched him walk away, and as he did so, he dropped the teddy on one of the ottomans. Anissa didn't know why, but he put a sick taste in her stomach. She waved for Gia to come take her place at the register. She needed something to drink.

Anissa went to the other side of Groove to get a glass of punch. She poured a glass and downed it within seconds. Still, she couldn't get the nasty taste out of her mouth. Why had Leon shown up like that? She hoped that he wouldn't make shopping at Groove a habit. That was one face she could go without seeing.

Brynn had been busy overseeing some feed-in braids Ru was putting in a young girl's hair, but one look at Anissa told her something was wrong. Within seconds, she was next to her at the punch table. "What's wrong? They working you that hard over there?" she asked, brushing a curl out of Anissa's face.

"Yeah, they are, but that's not a problem. I don't mind making money."

"Then what's the problem? You're looking like somebody stole your puppy."

"Leon just stopped by."

"What?" Brynn stopped moving. "Have you talked to him recently?"

"No. Not since that night. He reached out to me a few times, but I never responded."

"That's weird," Brynn noted.

"Yeah, he just walked up to me like he wanted to buy something."

"Well, he is a pimp. Maybe he was shopping for his hoes."

"He didn't buy anything though." Anissa shook her head and placed her cup down. "I don't think he even had an intention of buying anything."

"He probably was just fucking with you." Brynn shrugged. "Don't take it too seriously. You know men's egos get hurt when they get rejected. And not only did you tell him no to going into business with him, he never even got to see what that pussy is like. He missed out and he knows it. So fuck him!"

"Maybe you're right," Anissa sighed. "But I hope his ass doesn't make showing up here a regular thing."

"If he tries that, I won't have any choice but to light his ass up." Brynn winked at her and patted her purse. "Now come on, dance with me! This night is about us!"

Even though she wasn't in the mood to anymore, Brynn was right. And she wasn't going to let Leon take something she'd worked so hard for. Soon, he was in the back of her mind, and the smile was back on her face as she moved her body to the DJ's mix.

Leon had done well hiding his frustration inside of Groove. If there was one thing he hated, it was losing, and next to losing it was not getting his way. And Anissa wasn't letting up. He got in his Mustang and drove off from the establishment, but not before peering in one last time and watching her dance. She was the piece of his collection that he was missing, and he had to have her.

He blamed himself for losing her in the first place. He introduced her to the true him too soon. He hadn't gotten into her mind yet. Every good pimp knew that to control the body, one must first control the mind. He could have just let it go and found a different girl, but there was no other like Anissa. She was perfect.

He wasn't even supposed to stop at Groove's. He was on his way to pick up his girls from one of their appointments. However, he just couldn't stay away. It had been over two months since he'd seen Anissa's face, and it was one he thought about every day. He didn't know what kind of spell she had over him, but it was powerful.

He drove for a little while before finally pulling into the parking lot of the hotel he'd dropped CoCo and Angel off at. Harmony was at home, sick. Normally he wouldn't have cared about that, but she was throwing up everywhere, and he couldn't have her doing that on his paying customers, so she got lucky that night. The gentleman that evening had only paid for an hour of fun, and that hour was over. It was time to pay up.

He walked in the hotel and made his way to the third floor to room 323. As soon as he got to the door, he heard CoCo inside cursing somebody out. Instantly, the hairs on the back of his neck stood up. He knocked on the door and waited for someone to open it.

"Who the fuck is it?" a gruff voice asked.

"It's Leon. I'm here for my Delights."

The door opened, and Leon walked in, letting the door shut behind him. It smelled like hot sex and sweat inside the room, and both queen-sized beds were badly disheveled. Leon looked at the two big white guys and at his girls sitting at the table. They were fully dressed but had angry expressions on their faces, especially CoCo.

"Well, it looks like everybody had a good time tonight," Leon said, offering a grin to the men's solemn faces. "Now it's time to pay the piper."

The men looked at each other, but before they could speak, CoCo did. "They said they wasn't paying us shit, daddy," she told him. "But with all that we did, they owe fifteen hundred each!"

"Is that right?" Leon said, looking from one man to the other.

"We're not paying them whores fifteen hundred dollars, man," the white guy with blond hair said and poked his chest out.

"And *this* is why I don't take on new clients. We went over the prices before I left," Leon reminded them with an even tone. "If you had no intention of paying, then you shouldn't have touched my girls."

"Like I said," the guy started again and took a step toward Leon, "we aren't paying shit. And if you don't like it, do something about it, boy."

The word "boy" triggered Leon's anger. Blond Hair didn't even know what happened to him, because in a split second, Leon had laid him out on the ground with one hit. His nose was busted, and blood gushed everywhere. The other guy tried to rush Leon but caught a fist to the gut and an uppercut to the chin when he doubled over. When both of them were on the ground, Leon fished in their pockets and took out their wallets. Both were stuffed with cash, which made Leon even madder. They were purposely trying to be disrespectful, but it didn't surprise him. White men often tried to have a good time with black girls for free. They didn't feel like they were worth much, but Leon's girls were diamonds. And because of that, they earned all the money both of those jokers had. He threw the empty wallets back at them as they groaned where they lay.

"Just in case you try to tell anybody about this, remember I have messages and voice recordings of you soliciting these two women for sex. Good night, fellas," Leon said and waved for the girls to follow him.

When they got to the car, both of them got in the back seat, and he drove off in the direction of their home. When they got there, he parked and sat in the driveway. He used the moment to count the money he'd gotten from those two jokers.

"Five thousand dollars," he said, impressed.

"We did good, didn't we, daddy?" Angel asked from the back seat.

It wasn't until he heard her voice that he remembered he wasn't alone in the car anymore. He glanced back at their eager faces through the rearview and paused. "*I* did good. Remember that."

"I don't see you out here sucking no dick and getting fucked in the ass. But you get to keep all my hard-earned money. I want to start keeping some money. Otherwise—" CoCo snapped boldly, and her face instantly froze in regret of opening her big mouth.

Leon turned around and snatched CoCo up by the hair so fast that she choked on her next words. He yanked her up in the front seat by her roots, and when she was there, he smacked her so hard that her head hit the dashboard. When she looked up, her lip was busted, and she had tears in her eyes.

"Otherwise you gon' what, bitch? Huh? Tell me. What exactly are you gon' do? Leave me?" Leon taunted with a monstrous look in his eyes. Angel was in the back seat, trembling, and when all CoCo did was silently cry, he gave a short laugh. "Yeah, that's what I thought. You don't have nobody in this world but me. Remember that."

"I know, daddy," CoCo whimpered. "But . . . but you promised."

"I promised what?"

"Daddy, you said you were going to start giving us money."

"Do you think the bills pay themselves? Or that I just snap my fingers and all the designer shit you have just falls out of the sky? No. It doesn't. Me providing for you is the only payment you'll ever need. Who am I?"

"Daddy," CoCo sniffled.

"And what does daddy do?"

"Take care of his property."

"That's right. But I can't do that if you aren't doing a better job. Y'all are gon' have to start working harder around here. This"—he shook the money in his hands—"should be a regular night. Every night."

"Well, how are we supposed to make more money if you keep the prices the same?" CoCo asked and instantly shielded her face when Leon looked at her.

In truth, he really was going to hit her again. But then her words hit him. She was right. He couldn't charge more for the same whores. He needed a new attraction, something to make what he already had more appealing. Something top of the line. He needed Anissa.

"You let me worry about that."

Chapter 7

The next few weeks consisted of nothing but work and more work. Anissa was starting to understand why bosses hired employees to do all the work. However, she wasn't ready to cut her pie into that many pieces yet. She also wasn't above putting in the labor for something she wanted. So far, she, Gia, and Alexus had been able to handle the continuous shipments and customers, but she could tell that they were getting exhausted working every day from noon to six. The money she paid was good, but still Anissa knew that she would need to stay open longer and have more support.

In all the beautiful chaos, Anissa realized that she hadn't spent much time with Brynn. As ironic as that sounded, given the fact that they worked in the same building and lived in the same home, they were always so busy. And when they were at home, they were either asleep or just doing their own thing with their "me" time. Which was why Anissa thought it would be good to finally get out to Sunday brunch on Groove's closed day.

Loelle's was packed when Anissa and Gia got there, but thankfully Brynn and Ru had already grabbed them a table. Ru was rocking a beautiful aqua blue bob-cut wig, and her makeup was beat. If you didn't know she wasn't born a woman, then you wouldn't unless she told you. She'd gotten a Brazilian butt lift and breast implants, but her face didn't need any work. She was gorgeous. Brynn was sitting beside her, looking effortlessly flawless as usual with two long braids in her hair.

"Hey, sistas!" Ru waved her fingers when she saw Anissa and Gia approaching. "Looking fabulous as usual."

"Oh, you like this? I got it from that new spot, Groove. Maybe you've heard of it?" Anissa teased, twirling in her open-toe sandal heels.

"I see what you did there," Brynn grinned and stood up to give her cousin a hug.

"I don't know why it feels like forever since we've kicked it," Anissa said, squeezing her tight before leaning in and giving Ru air kisses. "And how are you, Miss Thing? I heard you got a new boo."

"*Another* new boo." Gia raised her eyebrows when she sat down across from Ru.

"Girl, I know you ain't out here telling my business," Ru said, jerking her head playfully at Gia.

"Bitch, I don't have my own, and your shit be juicy, okay?" Gia laughed.

"Okay, hold on. Let's order our food before she gets into this tea," Anissa said. "Fucking with Ru's ass, I'ma need something to drink, because I know the story is gonna leave a bitch thirsty."

"Okay! What was it last time? That nigga had you bent over the high-rise balcony?" Brynn asked.

"Ooh, baby, yes. That was Donald. I miss his fine ass," Ru said, pursing her lips and closing her eyes like she was lost in a memory.

They all laughed, and Anissa waved the waitress over to them to let her know they were ready. After placing their orders and getting their bottomless mimosas, they turned their attention back to Ru. She pretended that she didn't see all of them looking at her as she sipped her mimosa. When the others didn't let up, she sighed.

"Okayyy! Ugh, y'all so nosy, but whatever. I'ma fill you hoes in, so listen up, 'cause it's story time, bitches."

Brynn raised her brows at Anissa, who cracked up. Ru was a mess, and that was exactly the reason Brynn had hired her. She brought life into the shop, and she was constantly on the boutique side of Groove shopping and talking Anissa's ears off. So she knew this story was going to be something else.

"Okay, so y'all know I had to drop Robert's ass like a bad habit," she started. "He was just too clingy for me, and I didn't like that. Nigga, you are six foot. I cannot be dragging your heavy ass around everywhere with me just 'cause you got trust issues."

"Don't say 'dragging,' now," Brynn said, giving her a look.

"Well, that's what it felt like! Shit, that muthafucka was smothering me. In the beginning, it was cute. But then I was like, you got to find you a hobby or something. Next!"

"And she don't be playing with that 'next' shit," Gia commented.

"Okay," Anissa agreed, and they slapped hands.

"Sure don't," Ru said. "Miss one next fifteen one coming! Bow bow. And that's exactly what happened. I wasn't even expecting to meet this dude, but things happen in mysterious ways. His name is Dexter. I was at the club, and he just walked up on me and told me he just had to get to know me. Next thing I know, he had me buck-naked in his hot tub, licking whipped cream from my nipples and sucking my dick."

Anissa almost spit out her drink. She wasn't ready for that ending, but she should have known better. With Ru she should always expect the unexpected.

"Ever since, we've just been talking every day. And when this crazy bitch right here doesn't have me working in the shop like crazy, we spend all our free time together. There's only one thing though."

"What?" Anissa, Brynn, and Gia asked in unison.

"He's married." Ru folded her bottom lip and looked away from them.

Anissa and Brynn just exchanged a glance but didn't say anything. They were the last ones to judge anybody about dealing with married men, but they also weren't going to say that. Nobody at Groove knew about their past, and it was going to stay like that. Gia, on the other hand, had an earful to say.

"Uh-uh, girl. Now that's wrong." Gia shook her head at Ru. "He's the one you need to drop like a bad habit."

"And why is that, honey?" Ru challenged.

"He's married for starters."

"Well, if baby girl was doing her job, then he wouldn't have come to me."

"Girl, all I'm saying is, on the wife's behalf, that's fucked up. Not only is he cheating on her, but he's doing it with a—"

"With a what? Because I'm all woman, honey."

"If that's the case, then why was he sucking your dick?" Gia said with a smirk, and soon after, they all started laughing.

"You know what? Fuck you, bitch," Ru said, patting the tears from her eyes from laughing so hard. "It is a new day and age out here. I understand where you're coming from, I really do. But just let me live my life. If I get my heart broken, I get it broken. I'll put it back together again, believe that. But he is not happy in his marriage, and I see it. We have fun together, and I like him. I just want to see where it goes. However, I know that in a few months, if that divorce ain't final—"

"Choo chooo." Anissa made train noises.

"That's right! Next one coming!" Ru exclaimed.

At that moment, a fine gentleman approached the table. He was tall with smooth, creamy skin and had muscles that made him look very strong. Anissa's eyes ran across his light brown eyes, perfectly symmetrical nose, and full lips. It took her a moment to realize that he was doing the same to her, and she heard her girls giggling behind her.

"Excuse me. I ordered my food to go, but I just couldn't leave here without knowing your name," he said to her. His voice matched his physique: powerful and sexy.

"I'm Anissa, and you are?"

"I'm Kendall. Look, I don't mean to be rude and impose, but do you mind if I have your number? Or you can take mine," he added quickly. "I'm in a time crunch right now, but I would love to take you out sometime. That is, if you don't think this is completely creepy and want me to get away from you, like, right now."

"No," Anissa said, unable to keep the smile from coming to her face. She could tell that he was nervous, and she liked it. It meant he was genuine. She took out her phone and handed it to him. "Put your number in it. I'll hit you up."

"Cool," Kendall said and did as she said. When he handed her the phone back, he had a small but sexy smile on his face. "Nice to meet you, Anissa. I hope to hear from you soon. You ladies enjoy your food."

With that he left, and Anissa found herself watching him walk out of the restaurant. He was wearing workout clothes, and she wondered if he was on his way to the gym. She finally snapped out of her trance when she heard her name being called, and when she turned back to her people, they all had knowing smirks on their faces.

"That's how I was when Dexter came up to me in the club. Ooh-wee, you feel it, girl, don't you?" Ru asked, giving her an "mm-hmm" look.

"I don't know what you're talking about. He is just another guy," Anissa said casually and sipped her drink.

"Another guy my ass. That muthafucka was fooinee!" Gia said. "Nah, he was foine foine!"

"That nigga was so fine he could get his dick sucked from the back, two times!"

Gia and Ru slapped hands, and by then their food had arrived. Anissa was starving, and the moment the aroma hit her stomach, she couldn't wait to fill it up. Before they dug in, however, Gia held up her glass for a toast.

"To the best business owners in South Beach," she said and waited for them to join in.

Brynn was the last one to raise her glass, and Anissa could have sworn she saw her expression shift slightly. She didn't know what that was about, but she was still all smiles.

From where she was seated, she could see the outside patio perfectly. There were couples and families who had decided to dine out there, but Anissa's smile dropped when she saw somebody seated and glaring back at her. It was Leon. He was sitting alone at a table that had the perfect view of her. He looked angry. No, not just angry. Pissed off.

Anissa gasped and dropped her glass. It didn't shatter, but her drink spilled everywhere.

"Yo, Nissa. What the fuck?" Brynn said and snatched her purse before it got wet.

"I . . . I'm sorry. It was Leon. He was right th . . ." She pointed at where he had been, but he was gone.

"Nissa, there's nobody there," Brynn said, looking toward the empty table.

"Who is Leon?" Ru and Gia asked at the same time.

"This crazy pimp she thinks is stalking her. He wants to recruit her, but she told him no."

"A pimp?" Ru raised her eyebrow. "Nissa, what kind of shit are you into?"

"Brynn, he was right there," Anissa swore, ignoring Ru.

"If he had been there, he would still be there," Brynn snapped. "You spilled that drink all over me. Look at my pants."

"I'm sorry. I didn't mean it. But I swear I saw him."

"Yeah, I'm sure you did," Brynn sighed and got a napkin to dab her pants with. "Listen, maybe after he came to the shop, he got into your head or something. But there is nobody there."

Anissa wanted to tell her that it wasn't in her head but figured it would be no use. She had been the only one to see him. The table got quiet before Ru brought up the topic of her married man again. Anissa didn't say anything else. She just ate her French toast and bacon, wondering why Leon wouldn't leave her alone.

Chapter 8

When Leon had seen Anissa point in his direction, he quickly stood up and hid behind one of the waiters carrying a food tray on his shoulder. He used the man as a shield until he was able to make his exit from the restaurant entirely. Leon had been following Anissa for the past few weeks, learning her moves and routine. For the most part, all she did was work at the boutique. It seemed that she'd left the life of escorting behind her, which was fine with him for the time being. It meant no one was laying their hands on her body. However, when Leon had seen the man approach Anissa at the table in Loelle's, a rage was set ablaze inside of Leon. She had given the man the same smile she'd given Leon not so long in the past.

He'd almost lost his cool. She was making him crazy. That was more of a reason to get her on board and in line. She had a lot of nasty traits that he would have to yank out of her, like her smart mouth, but she didn't know the rules yet, so she got a pass.

After Leon left Loelle's, he made a very important stop. Anissa wasn't the only one with business ambitions. In fact, for the past five months, Leon had been getting his own building renovated. He pulled into the smooth, freshly painted parking lot and stared at the black building for a moment. It was located in a place on the outskirts of Miami, away from other neighborhoods and businesses. It used to be an old warehouse for used parts, but now it looked like a completely different place. The words FANTASY HOUSE were on top of it in black letters, but once it was lit up, it would shine a bright neon purple. It was listed as a gentlemen's club, but it would be far more than that.

Leon knew that brothels were illegal where he was, but so was selling drugs. People still sold and bought those, so why should pussy be any different? Not just anybody would be able to get inside the Fantasy House. A person would have to be a member holding one of three membership card statuses: silver, gold, or white, white being the most elite. The status determined what kind of perks each member would be able to indulge in. He'd gotten the idea from a similar club in Miami that had closed down. The only things he needed were more girls and a main attraction. CoCo, Harmony, and Angel were busy recruiting that moment. He wanted to be up and running by the next month. They were told that if they didn't come back with two girls each who were up to par with his standards, they wouldn't eat for a week. As far as the main attraction, he was still working on it. He figured he would try one more time to get Anissa on the winning team.

After Leon sat outside of the Fantasy House for another hour lost in his thoughts, he decided it was time to go put his plan into action. That first night at the club, Leon had thought Anissa would be an easy target. She had continuously been proving him wrong. He figured that if Anissa did what she had done the past two Sundays, he knew exactly where he could find her.

When he pulled his car in front of Groove, he saw that he had been right. He spotted her Audi parked in the back before he peeped her through the window doing inventory. He got out and went inside.

"You know, you should really lock that door if you ain't open today, shawty."

Anissa jumped at the sound of his voice. She'd been in the middle of pulling dresses out of a cardboard box so she could hang them up. When she stood up straight, she looked frantically around until Leon saw her eyes fall on her purse. He put his hands up as if to tell her to calm down. Still, she held tightly on to a metal hanger, positioning it in front of her.

"I come in peace," he said and flashed her a charming smile.

"What the fuck were you doing at Loelle's earlier?" she asked.

"Loelle's?" Leon faked confusion. "I wasn't at Loelle's earlier."

"You're lying! I saw you. You were staring at me with this creepy look on your face."

"Nah, wasn't me. But you probably have a plethora of niggas out here sniffing behind you," Leon told her and licked his lips.

"You need to leave, Leon. I don't want you here."

"You don't even want to hear the reason I popped up like this?"

"No!"

"I don't really like that word," Leon told her seriously, but she didn't seem to care.

"Well, get used to it coming from my mouth."

"I'd rather hear something else coming from your mouth," Leon said with a chuckle. "Something like my name in a high-pitched moan."

"That's never gonna happen," Anissa spat.

"Don't be so sure."

"What are you gonna do, force me?"

"I wouldn't have to force you. Women listen to me when I give commands."

"Oh, yeah, because you're a pimp, right? You have all the bitches around you brainwashed."

"I wouldn't brainwash you," Leon said and looked around her establishment. "I mean, look at what you've done for yourself. You clearly are a strong woman. You know, shawty, I never asked. How did you pay for all this? Business startups usually take some major coin, and you and ya cousin jumped out of the gate running."

"Fuck you, Leon."

"Oh, you weren't fucking me," Leon laughed. "But you was fucking somebody. So, the way I see it, you and me ain't so different."

"I would never work for you, Leon," Anissa said, rolling her neck. "I know that's what you're here for. And it's not gonna happen. I'm done with that life, but even if I weren't, I would never put myself in a position to give a nigga all of my paper."

"What if I said I could put you in a position to make more than what you made on your own and more than what you make here in your little store? There is something about you that I can't shake. And if I, a man who has experienced and seen every kind of woman, can't shake you, then I know you have to be a moneymaker. I want you on my team. Nah, I need you on my team. You can still have your store. Double the money. Together we can be unstoppable. You can be my queen. You used to smile when I called you that. I'm not tryin'a take all your money, just a little ten percent. Just like an agent would take as his fee. Think about it."

"Nigga—"

"Shawty, please, just think about it," Leon said. "That's all I'm asking you to do."

"You gon' stop stalking me? 'Cause that shit is weird. I don't like that."

"I don't know what you're talking about. I was handling business all morning. I'll be hearing from you soon."

With that, Leon turned and left. Did he know she only told him what he wanted to hear to get him out of her store? Yes. Did he care? No. He'd planted the seed. Now all he needed to do was create a need for himself.

Chapter 9

"Hey, what ya doing?"

At the sound of Anissa's voice, Brynn jumped. She had been so into what she was doing that she hadn't heard the front door to the condo open. She had been sitting at the island going over some paperwork, but upon Anissa's entrance, she hurried to jumble it all together.

"Oh, hey. Nothing much." Brynn shrugged. "How did it go at the shop?"

"Fiiine," Anissa said, giving her cousin a weird look. "Why are you acting so strange?"

"I'm not. You just scared me," Brynn said, trying to laugh it off.

"Uh-huh. What are you looking at?" Anissa asked, trying to peek over Brynn's shoulder, but she covered the papers with her hands.

"None of your business," she said. "You're so nosy, do you know that?"

"I've been told that once or twice," Anissa said and went straight to the fridge. "Do we have anything to eat? I left my leftover Loelle's at Groove by accident."

"Not anything that you don't have to cook. We can get some takeout if you want," Brynn told her, scooping the papers up and heading for her room.

"What about delivery? I don't want to leave again today."

"We can do that, too," Brynn called over her shoulder. When she came back, Anissa was propped on the living room couch seemingly lost in thought. "What are you thinking about?"

"Nothing," Anissa said, shrugging her thoughts off.

"Girl, bye. I know that look. Something is on your mind tough, so spill it." Brynn pushed Anissa's feet to the side and plopped down beside her.

"Have you had the thought of going back?"

"Going back to what?"

"Escorting."

"Um, I've been keeping so busy that I haven't even thought about it. So, I guess the answer is no," Brynn told her. "Are you thinking about it?"

"It crossed my mind. I mean, not going back, but just that if I did, I could be making double the money."

"But why would you do that when you're making good and legal money now?"

"The store has only made twenty thousand dollars so far. And with that, I have to pay employees, restock, and do a whole bunch of other miscellaneous shit. I'm technically still depending on my escort money in the background." Anissa sighed. "I wish I hadn't spent money so fast on stupid shit. I used to be able to make thirty bands in two weeks."

"So, you mean to tell me that instead of getting your hustle on and pushing yourself to hit that same goal with Groove, you would rather go back to selling your body?"

"I mean, I did it before."

"But now you don't have to. Always go forward, never back. Give Groove a chance. I need you to."

"Okay." Anissa gave a fake groan, and Brynn laughed.

"Girl, don't make me get you. I'm about to take a shower. When I get out, let's get Chinese."

"Okay."

Brynn went to her room and grabbed some pajamas out of her drawer. Although it was still early, she had no plans of stepping out of the condo until she had to leave for work the next day. At first it was a weird thing, having to get up and go to work. She hadn't been on a schedule since she was in high school and worked at a shoe store in the mall. And even though she was the boss and could come in whenever she wanted, Brynn wanted to be disciplined. She didn't want to start her business off with bad, slacker habits. So, she set a real schedule for herself. That way, her hair clients would always know her availability.

Brynn turned on the water in her glass shower to the hottest she could stand before stripping out of her day clothes and putting on her shower cap. When she got in and shut the door behind her, she let the hot water comb down her body like lava. It felt so good, especially on her erect nipples. She was instantly turned on but pushed the thoughts of lust to the far back of her mind. It felt like it had been so long since someone had touched her body sexually, but that was okay. She'd had enough sex to last a lifetime. She wanted to cleanse herself, maybe even practice abstinence for a while. Either way, the next time she let someone touch her sexually, it would be because she felt love.

Brynn found herself humming in the shower as she cleaned herself. By the time she was done, the bathroom was so steamy it looked like someone had just hot boxed inside of it. She got out and wrapped herself in a towel before wiping the mirror so that she could see herself. She'd come a long way from being that foster child nobody wanted. Her past was something that she didn't talk about to anybody, not even to Anissa.

Brynn was sure it was assumed that she had been an escort because of the fast money, but in truth it was the only thing she could do to survive back then. Nobody wanted her: not her mother, she didn't know who her daddy was, and all her foster parents did was spend the state's check on getting high. So as soon as she was 18, she left Atlanta and everybody behind. She did what she had to do to eat. And yes, soon the money did get too good to turn away, but all of that was in the past now. She would never go back.

When she had dried off completely, applied lotion to her body, and gotten dressed, Brynn left the bathroom. A gust of cold air hit her moist face, but not before the sight of Anissa sitting on her bed did. Brynn opened her mouth to ask if Anissa was ready to order the food yet, but then she saw what was in her hands. She stopped in her tracks and felt like all the breath had left her body. When Anissa realized Brynn was standing there, she glared up at her with so much hurt in her eyes.

"Anissa . . ." she started, but no words followed.

"You know, I knew you were acting weird when I walked in." Anissa gave a small, spiteful laugh. "I haven't seen you jump like that since we were kids when my mom caught you stealing cookies. I guess my nosiness served me right this time, huh?"

"Nissa, I can explain."

"Explain what? These business papers?" Anissa waved the papers Brynn had been looking over when she walked in. "The business papers for Groove that don't have my name anywhere on them? It says here that you are the sole owner of both the salon and the boutique. It also says here that you got the company name 'Groove' registered to you, Brynn Hollingsworth."

"Anissa—"

"Bitch, you better stop saying my name and explain this shit to me. I don't remember you putting a dime in on anything inside of it. But what I do remember is giving you my portion of the money to get the Groove boutique registered under my name. You brought the papers to the building for me to sign."

Brynn was frozen, and a single tear dropped down her face. Anissa was staring at her big cousin for answers, and she got the one that she hadn't asked. It was all over her face.

"Brynn, what papers did I sign?" Anissa asked, standing up. "Brynn! What papers did I sign?"

"You signed a paper waiving all your rights to ownership of the business," Brynn finally said, blinking her tears away.

"Wh . . . what?"

"Anissa, I'm so sorry," Brynn said and tried to take a step to her, but she stepped back.

The look on Anissa's face was one of sadness, grief, betrayal, and anger mixed together. And Brynn couldn't blame her. At first, Brynn had every intention of making Anissa a real partner in Groove's legacy. But upon meeting with Jason to get the deed to the building, she told him her plans, and he advised her from a business perspective to get it all in her own name. He said going into business with people was a sticky situation, but if she planned on doing right by her cousin, everything would be fine. But it wasn't fine. One look at Anissa's expression was proof of that.

"How could you do that to me?" Anissa breathed.

"Cuz—"

"My time."

"Cuz, I—"

"My money."

"Anissa, I never meant to hurt you."

"How could you not? You're sitting up here talking about Leon being a pimp, but that's exactly what you're doing to me."

"It's not the same thing, Anissa."

"How is it not? You just did it the legal way. Every dollar of my money I spent on the boutique is gone because no matter how hard I work, every dollar I make back is legally yours. I trusted you, and you made me your ho. And I would have never known. You had me sign over the rights to my dream, Brynn. My *dream*. I ain't never wanted nothing else, and you took that from me. I can't even stand to look at you right now."

"Anissa—" Brynn tried to grab her by the arm before she could leave the room, but she jumped away.

"No! You stay the fuck away from me. I hate you! I don't care if I ever see your ass again."

"Wait," Brynn sobbed and ran into the hallway after her.

It was too late. Anissa had already grabbed her purse and was out the door.

Brynn knew she had made a big mistake, especially when Anissa didn't come home that night. She found that out by going in Anissa's room the next morning. The bed was still made from the night before, and nothing else seemed to be touched. Brynn thought that if she gave her cousin her space, then they would be able to talk like adults. She wanted to be able to explain to her that she never had any intention of keeping the money the boutique made. However, Anissa didn't show up to work that day either. In fact, the boutique stayed closed all day.

She ignored all questions of why Anissa wasn't there, holding on to the hope that she would come in. But that never happened. By the end of the day, Brynn felt like scum. Even more so because she hadn't even entertained the idea of legally giving Anissa half of the business. She didn't see why it mattered, because the building was in her name, and she didn't want Anissa to have to pay her every month to rent out the other side. So, she just said it was all hers. She would never turn her back on Anissa. Groove would always be both of theirs.

When her last client left, Brynn sat in her own chair lost in her thoughts.

"You okay, boss lady?" Tamar asked, cleaning her shampooing station before she left.

"Yeah, I'm good."

"I can't believe Miss Thing didn't show up to open today," Ru said through pursed lips as she organized her utensils. "Those customers were one word: pissed!"

"She's just dealing with something. She'll be here tomorrow," Brynn said.

"Well, she better be, because I would hate to have to beat up one of her customers. One of them bitches had the nerve to tell me to unlock the door so she could get a lingerie set for her man. I looked at that bitch and said, 'No. But send him my way, because I have plenty.'"

"Girl, you are a mess!" Tamar said, cracking up with Ru.

Brynn wasn't even in the mood to laugh. She was just ready to close the shop and leave. When Tamar and Ru were done straightening up their sections, they each gave Brynn a hug.

"We're about to head to the bar for a quick drink. You want to come?" Tamar asked.

"No. When I leave here, I'm going home to get into bed."

"All right, baby, we'll see you tomorrow."

When they left, Brynn sighed. She swiveled in her chair, turning her back to the door, and reached into her ivory Chanel bag to pull out her phone. She dialed Anissa's number but got sent right to voicemail. Not one to give up easily, she sent a text message.

I know you're mad at me right now, but I just want you to know I love you. No matter whose name is on paperwork, Groove is both of ours. No matter what happens between us, I would never stop your paper. Good or bad terms, I love you too much to ever do that. If you want, you can take Groove Boutique for yourself. I will have the paperwork drawn up. I hope you come to work tomorrow.

Right before she could send the message, she heard the door chime. Thinking Ru or Tamar had left something, Brynn spun around in her chair. Only it wasn't them. She dropped her phone when she saw who was standing there.

"What are you doing here? We're closed."

"Don't worry. I'm not here for a haircut. I'm good in that department," Leon said with a smile before rubbing the waves on his head.

"Anissa's not here," Brynn told him, getting to her feet. "She didn't come to work today."

"Then it's a good thing I'm not here for her."

"Then why are you here, Leon?" Brynn asked, taking a step back toward her purse, where her pistol was.

"You know what I realized? After Anissa kept shooting down my offer?"

"That you're a dirty piece of shit?" she spat.

"No. That's a good one though," he chuckled. "I realized that the way to get her to see my vision was to create a need for myself. You see, I also realized that the only thing standing in my way was this place. Groove. So, I looked into the deed of this building, and imagine my surprise when I didn't see her name anywhere on it."

"Exactly. This is my building," Brynn said, taking another step toward her purse. She was almost there.

"And do you want to know my last realization?"

"Not really, but I'm sure you're gonna tell me."

"This is true. You're funny," he said and then smiled sinisterly. "My last and final realization was that I was wrong. Groove wasn't the thing in my way of getting her. You are."

Brynn tried to make a quick grab for her purse, but three shots rang out before her hand even touched its straps. She felt burning in her thigh, her shoulder, and her stomach. When she looked down, she saw red circles starting to expand on her clothes. Her shocked eyes traveled to Leon, who was holding a smoking gun, and she realized that she had been shot. That was when the pain came. She dropped to the ground, suddenly unable to stay standing. Her breathing was rigid, and she knew that she was dying. Her body was growing weak by the second, and the darkness was closing in on her. The last thing she heard before things went completely black was Leon's voice.

"It didn't have to be like this."

Chapter 10

Anissa didn't know the last time she'd run so fast in her life. She couldn't breathe, not because she was out of breath, but because it felt like somebody had their hands wrapped around her throat. She burst through the hospital doors, and right before she could ask the receptionist where Brynn was, she saw Ru waving at her from the lobby. She was there with Tamar, Gia, and Alexus.

"Oh, my God, Anissa!" Ru sobbed, and the two of them embraced each other. "I went back to get my wallet, and she was just lying there, bleeding out."

"What happened?" Anissa said hoarsely through her tears when they broke away from each other. "Who did this to my cousin?"

"We don't know. And she wasn't getting the cameras installed on the building until next week. Oh, my God. It was bad, girl."

"What are they saying?"

"She's in surgery right now. Come on, sit down."

"No, I need to see my cousin." Anissa tried to pull away from her. It took all three of them to hold Anissa from rushing back to the OR. "Get off of me!"

She fought against them, screamed, and cried for ten minutes until she no longer had any energy left. They took her to a lobby chair, and she just stared into space. They tried to talk to her, but she didn't hear their words. It felt like her entire world had come crashing into her face. The numbness took over her body. Everything was a blur. All Anissa could think about was the last thing she'd said to Brynn.

"I hate you! I don't care if I ever see your ass again."

And now she might have gotten her wish. But she didn't mean it. If she could have anything in the world, it would be for Brynn to walk through those double doors with her big smile. Anissa was beating herself up, and the more she thought about things, the more tears fell. Brynn had always been there for her since they were little, and Anissa hadn't been there when her cousin needed her the most. Her heart was breaking every second, and she couldn't stand it.

She finally took a deep breath and tried to get it together. If Brynn could see her now, she would tell her to get her shit together and be strong.

To her right, a woman wearing a white doctor's coat approached them, holding a clipboard. She looked at all of them as if trying to decide which one to talk to. "Hello, I'm Dr. Sing. Are any of you next of kin for Brynn Hollingsworth?"

"Me. I'm her cousin. We're the only family each other has in Miami," Anissa said in a weak voice. She stood up and looked the doctor in the eyes, trying to find some information. "Is my cousin alive? Is she gonna make it?"

"The surgery was successful. We were able to remove all three bullets without damaging any major organs or causing any nerve damage, but Miss Hollingsworth lost a lot of blood. She's in a coma."

"How . . . how long will that last?"

"I wish I could tell you, but we don't know," Dr. Sing said with a sigh. "Her body suffered a lot of trauma. I've seen these kinds of comas last days, months, and sometimes even years."

"Years? So, you're telling me my cousin will be in a hospital bed unconscious for a year?"

"No, I'm not saying that she will be. I'm just saying be prepared for all possibilities. At this point, we are optimistic, but anything can happen. Right now, it is just a waiting game."

"Can we see her?"

"In just a moment. The nurses are getting her room ready."

"Okay. Thank you, Doctor."

Dr. Sing nodded her head and disappeared again. Anissa sat back down in her seat and tried to process the information. Brynn was alive, and that was the most important thing. Now there were other things to worry about. Anissa hadn't thought about what would happen if she weren't conscious.

"I'm just glad she's alive," Tamar said. "I feel like I can breathe again. But I still can't get the thought of her lying there like that out of my head. Who would do something like that to her?"

"I don't know," Ru said and looked at Anissa. "Does your cousin have any enemies?"

"Not that I know of," Anissa answered, racking her brain. "Just bitches hating on her on the 'Gram, but I'm sure none of them would bring that petty jealousy to real life."

"You never know. Bitches are crazy these days," Gia said. "Especially since she just opened her business. They would know where to find her."

"Excuse me," a deep voice interrupted their conversation.

Anissa looked up at a black man of average height in a nice tailored suit. He wasn't a bad-looking man, and his cologne made the hospital smell disappear for a moment in Anissa's nostrils. He opened his suit jacket and flashed a badge.

"Is one of you Anissa Burke?" he asked, and Anissa nodded her head and raised her hand. "My name is Detective Evans. Do you mind if I ask you a few questions about what happened tonight with Brynn Hollingsworth?"

"Go ahead," Anissa said, and he pulled out a notepad.

"Where were you at the time of the shooting?"

"I was at home, in my room."

"Do you have anyone who could corroborate that?"

"The building has cameras in every hallway. I'm sure you can verify that with the building manager."

"I sure will," Detective Evans said, scribbling something down.

"You're asking her that like you think she did it or something," Ru said in a smart-mouthed tone. "Brynn is that girl's cousin. She would never hurt her."

"It's okay, Ru. He's just doing his job. Better he get the bullshit questions out of the way so that he can do his job and find the person who shot my cousin. Isn't that right, Detective?" Anissa said, and she and Detective Evans held each other's gazes for a few seconds.

"Do you know anyone who would want to hurt Brynn?"

"No. She doesn't have any enemies."

"Is she in a gang?"

"What? No! Never."

"How did she get the money to open up her own business?" the detective asked, and Anissa scoffed.

"Why does that matter?"

"Because she's only twenty-eight and owns a building worth $250,000. Not rents, owns. She also owns a condo worth $100,000. Do you have any idea how she obtained that kind of money?"

"Maybe it was a gift," Anissa said, offering what was most likely the truth. She had no idea that the building Groove was in was worth so much money. She knew Brynn hadn't saved that much up. One of her tricks must have given it to her as a present. Anissa's best guess was that it was either Bill or Jason. They were her richest clients, but of course she couldn't tell the detective that.

He laughed at her words anyway. "Yeah, right. Is she involved in some sort of illegal dealings?" The detective saw how Anissa was looking at him after that question, and he sighed. "I'm only trying to help. I want to catch the person who did this as much as you want me to."

"Nah. I think you're trying to make my cousin out to be some type of stereotypical black person like your kind always does."

"My kind?"

"Yeah, sellouts. Get the fuck out of my face. I'm done with your questions."

"Fine." Detective Evans tucked his notepad away into his pocket. "However, I should inform you that since this is an active investigation, and until we can verify Miss Hollingsworth's income, we will have to shut down her place of business until further notice. Also, her home has now become an official part of our investigation."

"That's where I live too."

"Well, then I suggest you pack a bag and find somewhere to go."

"What? You can't close Groove! That's how we all make our money!" Ru exclaimed.

"Right! Nissa, tell him you own Groove too," Gia said, nudging Anissa. "Tell him!"

But she couldn't, because he knew just like she did that her name was nowhere on the deed to the building, or on any of the paperwork for Groove. Anissa didn't say anything. She just glared at him as he looked back at her with a smug expression.

Ever since Anissa was little, she had hated law enforcement. He hadn't come to help them. He'd come to burn Brynn at the stake even though she was the real victim.

What made it worse was that they shared the same ancestry, but that didn't matter to men like Detective Evans, as long as he was in the big house.

When he walked out of the hospital, she let out a frustrated shout. She walked away from them, swinging her arms.

"What are we gonna do now?" Ru asked, coming up next to her. She didn't care about Anissa's frustration. They were all frustrated.

"I don't know," she said.

"Anissa, you're gonna fight this, right?" Ru asked and looked into Anissa's puffy eyes.

"I don't know if that will even be possible," Anissa whispered.

"Girl, I know you're hurting, but Brynn would want you to keep Groove going," Ru pressed.

"Brynn never even wanted me to have a piece of Groove."

"What do you mean? You own the boutique next to her salon."

"Yeah, I thought I did too, until yesterday when I was looking at the paperwork and didn't see my name anywhere on it. The licensing papers I thought she had me sign were really papers signing over my rights to my own boutique."

"Brynn wouldn't do that." Ru shook her head.

"Well, she did it. I saw it with my own two eyes. That's why I didn't come to work today. I was just so mad. My last words to her last night were that I . . ." Anissa choked up and had to close her eyes so more tears wouldn't fall. But they fell anyway. She turned her face up and sniffled, trying to hold in a sob. "I told her I hated her, and now she's in there fighting for her life. And I don't have the business anyways."

"Come here, honey," Ru said, and pulled Anissa into a tight embrace. "None of this is your fault. Any of us would have been upset finding out something like that. Just don't tell that rinky-dink detective that, or he's gonna think you had something to do with this."

"Okay," Anissa whispered.

At that moment, a nurse came back to get them from the lobby and told them they could go back to see Brynn. Ru tried to link her arm with Anissa's so that they could walk together, but Anissa stepped back. She shook her head and motioned for Ru to go on ahead of her.

"I'll be back in a second. I have to prepare myself to see her looking like that."

"Okay, baby. Take all the time you need. I love you, and I'm here for you." Ru gave Anissa another hug before walking back with the others.

When they were gone, Anissa took a big breath. Seeing Brynn lying in a hospital bed hadn't exactly been in her things to do. It was something she thought she would never have to see, unless maybe she decided to have a baby. Now what if she couldn't even have babies? Or a future? What if the doctor's theory was right and she didn't wake up? Brynn didn't have any close family, and neither did Anissa. Anissa's mom was dead, and Brynn's might as well have been. What was she going to do without her right hand?

Her mind fell on Groove. It was her only source of income at the moment. She and Anissa had their cash stashed in a storage unit in South Beach, but that wouldn't last forever. And who knew how long Brynn would be out of commission? Anissa needed a way to make some major cash, enough cash for her to really open her own boutique and get her own place to stay. Because right then she was technically homeless. She thought about going back and doing her own escort thing, but then her mind fell on the one person she'd been trying to avoid.

Leon.

As much as she hated what she was about to do, she felt as if she had no choice. She needed somewhere to lay her head and a way to make some money. He had both.

She pulled out her phone and made the call. "Hey, Leon," she said when he answered. "It's Anissa."

Chapter 11

"Whoa, whoa. Slow down, honey. Slow down!"

Anissa looked up to see one of Leon's girls, Angel, rushing into the bedroom she'd been given. A few days had passed since Brynn had been shot, and she hadn't left the room once. Instead, she'd been in there sulking day in and day out about her cousin and drowning her sorrows in a bottle of Jack. When she was drunk and numb, she didn't feel anything. And that was the way she liked it. Angel snatched the half-empty bottle away from her and hid it behind her back when Anissa tried to grab for it back.

"No!" Angel said.

"Just give me the bottle. You don't give a fuck about me."

"You're right, but that's only because I don't know you. But you're family now, so I can't just let you kill yourself with alcohol poisoning."

"What's it to you?"

"Like I said, you're family. And you're very important to daddy, so—"

"So what? You don't want to get your ass kicked if something happens to me when he left me in your care?" Anissa said with a laugh, but Angel didn't laugh with her. In fact, she held a serious expression that let Anissa know that was exactly what would happen. "He . . . he puts his hands on you?"

"Not all the time. Only when he's angry."

"And is he angry a lot?"

"He's angry enough."

"Yeah, well, he's not gonna do that to me."

Angel opened her mouth as if she wanted to say something but closed it just as quickly. She placed the bottle on the ground and sat next to Anissa on the bed. Angel gave her a look of sadness and pity.

"I heard about what happened to your cousin," she started. "I'm sorry. That is very sad. Everyone in this house has dealt with great loss and sadness. But the one thing that you don't want to do—no, that you *can't* do—is depend on something to take away the pain. Life doesn't work that way."

"And why doesn't it?" Anissa slurred.

"Because if the calm isn't natural, the storm always comes back. Once you sober up, the pain will still be there. Don't fall victim to it. Allow yourself to feel it and you can control it. If you don't, it will destroy you. Especially here."

Her words hit Anissa directly in the chest. "What are you, some sort of counselor?"

"I used to be, a long time ago." Angel nodded.

"Then how'd you end up selling pussy for Leon?"

"My daughter died."

"I'm sorry to hear that."

"Don't be sorry. It wasn't your fault. Her father was driving her home after getting her from day care. He was rushing, driving too fast in the rain. He went around a bend too fast on the interstate and flipped the car. He survived. She didn't. My life was ruined. She was only two years old. You know the fucked-up part?"

"What?" Anissa asked, thinking she'd already heard that part.

"The fucked-up part is that he wasn't trying to rush home to be with me. He was rushing to drop her off to me so that he could be with another woman. The same woman he left me for two weeks after we put Elana into the ground."

"Damn," Anissa said, shaking her head. "That's fucked up."

"I told you," Angel said with no emotion. "I didn't have anybody. I was so depressed that I lost my job, and my house was soon to follow. When Leon found me, I had literally hit rock bottom. He told me that the world needed a beauty like me to be up and never down. He promised me a good life and that he wouldn't hurt me like Elana's father did. I believed him and let him bring me here. I've been here ever since.

"I was his second girl. CoCo was his first. He made me feel special, and I wanted to do something to repay him for his kindness. I saw how CoCo made him happy, so I just did what CoCo did. I didn't have anything else, and now I have everything. So what if I have to sleep with somebody from time to time? Leon makes sure that they're clean, so our health stays intact, and he makes sure we have everything we could ever want."

"Sounds like you're trying to sell him to me," Anissa told her and fell back onto her new, soft bed. Her head was spinning.

"No," she barely heard Angel say before her eyes closed. "That was then. He's different now."

Anissa was asleep, and by the time she woke up, she wouldn't remember that part of the conversation. She had dreams of Brynn's face when she told her she hated her. Then the dream flipped to Brynn in the hospital bed, only she wasn't alive. She had bullet holes in her chest. Anissa screamed and tried to reach out to her, but the more she reached, the farther away Brynn got. She began yelling Brynn's name over and over until she felt a hard jerk.

"Anissa!" someone shouted.

"Brynn!"

"Anissa!" the voice shouted again, and she felt her body jerk once more.

Her eyes flew open. Her surroundings were a blur, and she saw two of everything until she blinked feverishly. She suddenly became aware that someone was holding her. When she looked, her eyes fell on Leon's face.

"You were shouting in your sleep, shawty. You good?" he asked, letting her go.

"I . . . I must have had a nightmare," Anissa told him. "I'm fine now."

"All right," he said, eyeing her suspiciously. "You were saying your cousin's name. Have they found out yet who did that to her?"

"The detective called me the other day, but he didn't want anything but to ask me more questions about where Brynn got all her money. They haven't found the person who shot her yet though."

"Well, if they do, tell me. I need my eyes peeled back sharp if someone is going around hurting beautiful women," he said, reaching to stroke her cheek, but she moved away. He smirked slightly and gave a small nod. "How about you get cleaned up and meet the rest of us downstairs for breakfast."

"What if I don't want to?"

"It wasn't a question," he said. "Plus, I have good news I want to share with everyone, and it won't be worth telling if you aren't there."

He didn't say anything else before he left the large bedroom and shut the door. She stretched and yawned big. Upon smelling her bad breath, she closed her mouth quickly. It smelled strongly of liquor and vomit. She got up from the bed and went to one of the many suitcases she had packed to grab something to throw on for the day. She then went to the bathroom so she could shower and brush her teeth.

By the time she was done and dressed in a flower sundress, she almost looked like herself except for the sadness in her eyes. After she'd placed her hair in a bun, she slipped on a pair of slippers Leon had gotten for her that had the letter A on them, and she left the bedroom.

The upstairs of the house was even bigger than what she had thought. There were at least eight bedrooms, not including the ones on the first floor. She made her way to the circular staircase, and once she bounded down them, she followed the scent of bacon.

Everyone she'd already met was in the kitchen, and CoCo was standing over the stove, frying bacon and sausages. Upon seeing her, Harmony waved, and Angel smiled her way. Leon sat at the end of the table and motioned for Anissa to sit next to him.

"I want my queen to sit to the right of me," Leon said. "CoCo, serve Anissa her food after mine."

"Yes, daddy," CoCo responded. "What do you want on your plate, boo?"

"Ummm . . ." Anissa looked around as everyone stared at her like she was a spectacle. "French toast, eggs, and bacon?"

"Coming right up."

"CoCo is the best cook in the house," Leon told her.

"That's . . . cool," Anissa responded and looked down at her thick thighs.

To them the atmosphere was normal, but for her it was the most awkward scenario she'd ever been in. They were like a fucked-up version of *The Brady Bunch,* and now she was part of it. Temporarily, anyway. CoCo did as she was told and served Anissa her plate right after Leon's and then sat down next to Angel toward the end of the eight-seater table. Anissa took note that the other girls didn't have their food yet.

"I didn't mean to take so long in the shower. Y'all must have already eaten."

"They don't eat until I tell them to eat," Leon said simply, and he dug into his plate.

"What?"

"They don't eat unless I tell them to," he repeated.

Anissa looked at the three women eyeing her plate hungrily, and Anissa could tell that what he was saying was true. She studied each of their faces, waiting for one of them to contest his words, but they didn't. They just sat there, sitting up straight like obedient little children. Anissa's gaze fixed on the fading bruises on the parts of their bodies she could see. None of them were fresh, but they were there, nonetheless. CoCo was the worst. She had marks on her neck, like she'd been choked. Also, it was obvious that her eye had been blacked recently. Anissa bit the inside of her mouth and averted her eyes to Leon, who had continued to eat his food.

"You aren't gonna tell them they can eat?" Anissa asked.

"When I feel like it."

"Okayyy." Anissa pushed her plate away from her. "Then I'll wait until then to eat too."

He stopped chewing, and it got so quiet in the kitchen that a pin could be heard dropping. Slowly, he looked up from his plate and was met with Anissa's eyes staring back at him. She saw a vein in his right temple protrude but then go back down. She didn't care if she was getting on his nerves. She saw that he clearly had no trouble putting his hands on women, but that didn't scare her. She would light his ass up if he ever thought he would physically hurt her. One thing men often used against her was her age. They thought that since she was young, she was impressionable. But Anissa, unlike the other girls at the table, had her own mind. And it wasn't going to be corrupted by the likes of Leon. She would never be like Angel, Harmony, or CoCo. She loved herself too much. Plus, she owed it to Brynn to remain strong while she was down.

"CoCo was kind enough to make your plate. They are good hoes. They know their place. You can eat," Leon commanded.

"No." Anissa's voice was strong. "Not until they eat."

"I don't think you understand how things work around here."

"I'm not about to eat in front of them if they are hungry. You might have their minds washed, but you don't have mine."

"Yet."

"Never. I asked for a favor: clients and shelter. Not to be pimped. I can go back to working for myself if I have to watch you treat them like shit. And I just want you to know, if you even think for one second that you're gonna be putting your hands on me, Leon, I will walk out that door right now."

"Then go. This is my house, my bitches, my rules."

"Fine."

Anissa stood up and made to go get her suitcases. She could stay in a hotel for the time being and contact some of her old clients. She was only able to take two steps before Leon spoke again.

"Wait," he said and sighed. When she turned back to him, he was looking at her with his fist clenched. His eyes never left her, but his next words weren't for her. "Make your plates and sit down. I have something to tell y'all."

Angel, Harmony, and CoCo moved quickly. It was almost as if they were trying to hurry and get food just in case he changed his mind. The visual hurt Anissa's heart so much that she was still contemplating leaving. She thought back to when Leon gave her butterflies. Now he just made her sick to her stomach. But she had to do what she had to do. She cleared her throat and sat back down in her seat.

"Are you happy now?" Leon asked her.

"Yes," she said, pulling her plate back in front of her.

"Now we can get to business," he said, looking around the table. "It's a shame that our new recruits didn't make it past preliminaries. I asked you three to find me the best, and you found me washed-up coke whores."

"Daddy, they looked the part. We thought you would be happy," Harmony said.

"They were junkies. All of them. And I don't need anyone on my team who has an addiction to anything but money and me."

"You don't let them use?" Anissa asked, openly shocked.

"No," he told her. "Not even weed. Drugs make you do stupid things. I need sharp minds around me. Alcohol use is only permitted in this house, never on jobs. When my girls are in the field, they have to be firmly on ten toes. The sex game has changed a lot these past years. Muthafuckas try to get away with not paying the ho, and some even try to hurt or even kidnap your girls."

"I thought that's what you're for, to stop that kind of shit from happening."

"And I do, for the most part. But some shit you have to be smart enough to get yourself out of. And you can't do that if you're pumped up with poison. That shit makes you a liability. Do you do drugs, Anissa?"

"No. I mean, I drink, but that's it."

He nodded his head. It was weird, because what he was saying was exactly what Brynn had told her when she had come to South Beach. Anissa had been a heavy marijuana smoker when her mother died, but when she got to Florida, all of that changed.

"To be a bad bitch, you have to think like one. And to think like one, you don't need anything tainting your

thoughts. Clear your mind, and you can be a boss like me."

Those words of Brynn's often played in her head before she went on a date. Mainly because she did want to be like her. She wanted to have the money, the clothes, and the cars. But as Anissa sat beside Leon and listened to him, the only thing she could see were the similarities between him and her cousin. Brynn had never put her hands on Anissa, but she did set up a lot of her dates. How was Anissa to know whether she was taking a cut off the top? Had Brynn been her pimp? Her stomach turned, and suddenly she couldn't eat anymore.

"You all right, baby?" CoCo asked, seeing the look on Anissa's face. "You don't like the food?"

"No, the food is delicious. I just . . . I think I drank too much last night."

"Okay." CoCo gave her a smile and went back to scarfing her own food down.

"That's exactly the reason I only allow drinking in this house, and only sometimes at that," Leon said, surveying Anissa. "Can't have you getting sick on paying customers."

"That has never happened before."

"Tell me something, shawty. When you worked for yourself, how much did you make in a night?"

"Five bands."

"Well, you have to teach me whatever moves you got," Harmony said.

"Shit, me too," Angel agreed.

"Y'all don't make that much a night?" Anissa asked, taken back.

"Hell no. Maybe fifteen hundred if we're lucky now."

"Now? What does that mean?"

Harmony looked over at Leon before she just bent her head and went back to eating. Anissa glanced at Leon and saw the poisonous glare he was giving Harmony.

Although he was only looking at one of the girls, the others quickly fell in line. Anissa still wanted someone to elaborate, but something else came to the forefront of her mind.

"Wait." Anissa put her hands up and made a face at Leon. "I thought you said you could help me make more money than I already was making. How can you do that if they aren't even getting half of what a normal night is for me? *And* you want to take a fee out? Oh, hell no. I'm better off on my own."

"See, queen, that's where you're wrong. When I first met you, I knew you were high priced."

"How did you even know I was an escort? I'm sure none of my clients know you, and I never told you what I did."

"I guessed, and you never denied it." Leon shrugged. "And five bands is pretty up there. I can't even cap on that. But I can help you make more than you've ever dreamed of."

"I don't do more than one man a night," Anissa told him. "I'm not a whore. I'm a lady. And I will be treated as such."

"Whew!" Leon said, clapping his hands. "And that right there is exactly why I need you. Because with that attitude, you would only have to have one client a night unless you wanted more. With what I have planned for you girls, money will be rolling in. But I need you to teach my girls how to walk and talk just like you. I need you to teach them how to *be* you."

"Be me?"

"Yes. Be you. They view themselves as hoes, and men don't pay top dollar for hoes."

"They think of themselves like that because of you," Anissa told him like it wasn't rocket science. "If you treat them like shit, they'll think they're shit. I think highly of myself. Just because I sell my body doesn't make me any less of a woman than those around me."

"Which is what is gon' make you a hit at the Fantasy Factory."

"The Fantasy Factory?"

"A gentlemen's club that I'm opening up next month. It's gonna be the hottest thing in this fucking city. Only the ballers and the wealthy will be allowed memberships, and there will be a minimum stipend for all customers."

"You know people willing to pay a stipend for pussy?"

"There will be other amenities that they'll be able to dabble in. You won't need to worry your pretty head with that though."

"Drugs," Anissa guessed, and she didn't need for him to tell her she was right for her to know she was. It was the only thing it could be.

"Among other things," Leon told her. "And as long as my Delights keep making them want to renew their memberships, the reward will be grand."

"You aren't worried about being shut down? Aren't brothels illegal?"

"To the regular eye, the Fantasy Factory will be nothing but a place where men come to frolic and get away from their nagging wives. The silver members will get to come and indulge in free alcohol and watching pretty women twirl on poles. But for white card holders? They'll have access to the back room and all the drugs and pussy they can handle for the night. I already have a lineup of clients who are ready to purchase memberships and be a part of the men's club. This month and next month I'm conducting tours of the facility, but I'm sure these guys will be in. And I'm sure they will tell their friends about it. Especially if you whip these girls and a few others into shape."

"How much are we talking as far as the monthly stipend?"

"The stipend will only be for the white card members, and they'll be required to tip a minimum of twenty thousand dollars a month, which can be spread to any girl in the back room. Or it can all go to one girl. That will solely be up to you girls."

"And you won't keep it?"

"I'll take my fee, of course."

"Not out of my earnings you won't."

"Excuse me, shawty. Repeat that. I didn't quite hear you correctly."

"You heard me, Leon. First let me say that actually sounds like a good idea, and I think it could work. But it still is sounding like you need me more than I need you. Not only do you want me to pretty much be your headliner, but you need me to get these bitches and others into shape. That's a lot of work. And I'm not paying you to work. If I come under the Fantasy Factory, I need it in writing that I will get to keep one hundred percent of my tips. Otherwise, it's a no-go. Not only that, but I want to pick my own set schedule, and if you ever lay a hand on me, all of our business is done. Do we have a deal?"

Leon's jaw clenched as her words resonated with him. She could tell that he thought she was just going to go along with being part of the gentlemen's club with no rebuttal. However, after what had taken place with Groove, Anissa knew exactly how important paperwork was. She wouldn't make the same mistake twice. She felt bad for the other girls, because she knew he would keep most of their money, but that was more of a reason for him to give her all of hers. She had to focus on number one: herself. She didn't want to work for Leon longer than she had to.

"Deal," Leon finally said, and Anissa smiled. "But until then I don't need you out in these streets working alone. You're no good to nobody if something happens to you."

"Perfect."

***

The soft crooning of Marvin Gaye played in the background as Leon leaned back on a black leather couch in his bedroom. His arms were propped up and spread-eagle while his neck and head rested on the cushion. His eyes were closed, and he was lost in his thoughts. Anissa had played a good game at breakfast that morning. Normally back talk boiled his blood, but when it came from her, it turned him on. He had been right about her. She was different. Smarter. But something she'd said when they first met played over in his head.

"I'm only loyal to myself."

He believed her, but that didn't mean it couldn't change. The thought of bending her to his will made his dick rock hard, which was why it was a good thing he had CoCo naked in front of him on her knees with it in her mouth. He did his best thinking when he got head, and CoCo had the best around. She was so good at it that she rarely used her hands. Her mouth and tongue did all the work.

He opened his eyes and looked down at her as she worked her pretty, full lips around his monster shaft. She was his first girl, which meant she'd been having sex with him the longest. She knew best how to please him, what made his toes curl. She forced him to the far back of her throat and made herself choke before slurping all the way back to his tip.

"You know what daddy likes, don't you?" he asked, and she nodded. He grabbed his rock-hard meat and took it out of her mouth. "Lie on your back."

She did as she was told on the cold wooden floor. He eyed her sexy body and licked his lips at her full breasts as he stroked himself. She lifted her legs up and opened them, giving him the perfect view of her glistening kitty.

"You like daddy's new business idea?" he asked her.

"Yes, daddy. I like all your ideas."

"You plan on working hard for me?"

"I always work hard for you, daddy."

"What you gon' do if somebody says they want to pee on you?"

"I'll tell them they aren't allowed to."

"And what do you say if daddy wants to pee on you?"

"I'll tell daddy that I'm his property, and he can do whatever he likes."

"That's what daddy likes to hear," Leon said, aiming the tip of his dick at her.

He didn't have much urine in his bladder, but what was there he sprayed out all over CoCo's body. The moment she felt the hot liquid on her, she moaned and rubbed herself all over. Although his girls sold themselves to make him money, there were still certain things that he would only allow for him to do to them. After all, they were his property, and some perks should be saved for him. Leon had always been a freak in the bedroom. Seeing her with his pee all over her turned him on and made him hornier than he was before. He loved knowing that he owned her and she would let him do anything he wanted to her. She would accept it, and she would love it. That was power.

When he was done, he made her turn around on her knees so that he could penetrate her love box from the back. When he slid inside, he threw his head back. He didn't know what CoCo did to keep it so tight, but it felt like heaven. Leon gripped her hips tightly so that she wouldn't run while he drilled into her. At first her love cries were from pleasure, but then they turned to whimpers of pain. He tuned her out and concentrated on his nut. Right before he exploded, he withdrew himself from her vagina and shoved his manhood into her asshole. She jumped, but he held her tight as he dug deep until he was completely inside and erupted like a volcano.

"Shit!" he shouted and threw his head back with his mouth open until the feeling subsided.

Underneath him, CoCo was shaking from the pounding he'd just given her. He wasn't even sure if she had climaxed, but he didn't care. She was there to please him, not the other way around. The look of lust was gone from his eyes, and he turned his nose up at her.

"Clean my floor up, and then go do something with yourself. You smell like piss."

"Yes, daddy," she said.

She stood up on shaky legs and went into the bathroom of his master bedroom and got a towel and cleaning spray. He sat back down on the couch, still naked from the waist down, and reached into the glass drawer next to him. From it, he pulled a Cuban cigar and sparked it. He took a few draws as his quick heart rate slowed, and he watched her clean the floor. His mind traveled to a place he hadn't been in a while: his childhood, his father, the man who had created the man Leon now was.

"You're a very special boy, do you know that?"

10-year-old Leon looked up into the pretty face of Tina, his father's girlfriend. She had always been nice to him. She was some years younger than his dad and had the type of body that made other men look whenever they were all out together. That always made Leon's dad mad, even though it wasn't her fault.

That night, she had tucked him into bed and had just read him a bedtime story. Tina always made time for him, even when his father didn't. Even when his dad was mean to her, she was always kind to Leon.

"My dad doesn't think so," Leon told her.

"Yeah, well, your dad is a tough one to please sometimes," she told him and went to the bookshelf in his race car–themed room to find another book.

The robe she wore over her nightgown slipped, and Leon caught a glimpse of her shoulder. Tina was fair skinned, but the bruise Leon saw was purple. He didn't have to ask how it got there to know.

"Why do you stay with him if he hits you?" he blurted out.

She turned to him and saw that he was looking at her shoulder. When she looked down and saw the bruise, she quickly fixed her robe and tightened it at the waist.

"You need to stay in a child's place. Don't be asking me them kinds of questions about me and your father. That's our business."

"Not really, if I have to hear it," Leon told her. "He hurts you almost every day, and you stay with us. Why?"

Tina gave Leon a sad smile and shook her head. "Because that's what you have to do when you don't got nobody or nowhere to go. You have to make do with what you have. Your father gives me food, nice clothes, and a beautiful home."

"So, you stay for the money?" Leon asked, and Tina scoffed.

"If you want to be technical, yes." She shrugged. "Yes. I stay for the money. And your dad has lots of it. And when you're his age, you'll have lots of it too because of him. So, play your cards right, you hear? Then you'll have women stupid enough to do whatever you say too."

She walked back over to the chair she'd been sitting in beside the bed with another book in her hand, The Catcher in the Rye. *He'd already read it, but he liked the story and didn't mind Tina reading it to him again. However, she only got through a page and a half before Leon's dad, Laron, burst through the bedroom door. He didn't even have to open his mouth for Leon to smell the booze expelling from his body. Laron surveyed the room first, like he was looking for something to be mad at, before his eyes finally fell on Tina.*

"Come to bed, Tina. I need you right now."

"Can I finish reading this book to Leon?"

"That muthafucka can read his own damn book! Now get your ass in that bedroom."

"Yes, baby," Tina said, quickly shutting the book and placing it beside Leon.

When she got up and walked past Laron, she kept her eyes on the ground until she was out of the room. Laron glared at his son for a second before breaking into a chuckle.

"If that bitch's pussy weren't so good, I'd kill her for talking back," he said. *"Let me tell you something if I never tell you anything else. Women ain't nothing without a man. They're weak. Your mama learned that the hard way. Bitch left me because she forgot she needed me. Now she's on the streets, begging for scraps. But Tina, she's smart. She does what I say. A little sassy at times, but that ain't nothing to get in check. When you're older and get yourself a woman, all you gotta do is create a need for yourself, and you'll own her. Make her think she can't live without you, can't breathe without you, and she will never leave you. Take your ass to sleep, boy. I have company."*

"Yes, sir," Leon said, and his father left.

He tried to obey his dad. He really did. But there was too much banging going on down the hall. Leon hoped that his dad wasn't hurting Tina again. Curiosity got the best of him, and he climbed out of bed and left his room. He tiptoed down the hall to his father's bedroom, and when he got to the slightly ajar door, he took a breath before he peeked inside. He almost lost his mind when he saw what was going on. His father wasn't slapping Tina around. They were having sex, but they weren't alone. There was another black woman there with a body like Tina's. They were all naked and going at it.

Laron had Tina bent over in front of him as he took her from behind. Leon couldn't lie, he was a young boy and had definitely imagined what Tina looked like outside of her clothes a few times. But the actual visual was ten times better than the fantasy. It was even better than the women in the naughty magazines he had hidden under his bed. Her arch was perfect as Laron sexed her like a crazed animal from behind.

Leon's eyes were so glued on Tina as she took the sexual beating and on watching the nipples of her bouncing breasts brush against the sheets, he forgot about the other woman. She was lying on her back, rubbing the ball on her vagina.

"Lick her pussy, bitch. And lick it good or I'm gon' put this dick in your ass," Laron told Tina, and she did it without hesitation.

Tina buried her face in between the thighs of the other woman, who instantly began to moan. As Leon watched some more, he heard his father give out more commands and watched the women comply. They did things to each other that Leon hadn't even heard of, just because he told them to. Leon looked down and saw that his "thing" was poking out, and he realized it was time to go back to bed.

When he was back in his room, he grabbed a flashlight, some lotion, and one of his magazines from under the bed. As he got under his covers, he was breathing heavily because he needed to relieve himself badly. It didn't take long to do, and when he was done, he lay back, thinking about his father's words. Leon couldn't wait to be a grown-up and make women do whatever he wanted.

Leon took another drag of his cigar as he came back to reality. CoCo was done cleaning the floor and putting the supplies back where she'd gotten them from. His mind was on his father's words, just like they had been that night.

"When you're older and get yourself a woman, all you gotta do is create a need for yourself, and you'll own her. Make her think she can't live without you, can't breathe without you, and she will never leave you."

He'd already created a need for himself with all his girls. There was only one who felt that she could live without him. Even after what he'd done to her cousin, Anissa wasn't grateful that he'd taken her in. She had already threatened to leave, and Leon knew she could make it on her own. He had to break her down.

"CoCo?" Leon said as she walked past him to leave the room.

"Yes, daddy?"

"I need you to do something for me."

"Anything, daddy."

"Keep an eye on Anissa for me. Get as close to her as you can. I need to know what makes her tick."

CoCo paused slightly, but Leon was busy ashing his cigar and didn't see it. She caught herself quickly and nodded.

"Of course, daddy."

Chapter 12

Weeks passed in Leon's house, and without wanting to, Anissa was beginning to grow comfortable. Leon didn't treat her the way he treated the other girls. In fact, he made it a point not to. He called her the queen of the house and acted as if she were royalty. When the other girls had to get up and clean, she was able to lounge around and do nothing. When Leon forced them out to work, he took her to dinner. She often woke up to gifts next to her bed, just like that afternoon.

Anissa had been lying in bed all day, although she'd been up since the morning. The moment she opened her eyes, they fell on a small black Chanel bag sitting on top of its box on her nightstand. It was the third purse Leon had gotten her that week. She loved it, but she knew that his gifts didn't come without a price. She knew that she was going have to deliver on her end of the deal, and quite well, or else she didn't know what would happen. There was something about Leon that Anissa couldn't put her finger on. Something dangerous.

Knock! Knock!

"I'm asleep!" Anissa called out.

"Then how are you talking, silly?" Harmony's voice rang out, and she opened the door. She stepped inside Anissa's room, fully dressed in a pair of high-rise skinny jeans and a blue Versace shirt that was tied at the bottom. She tucked a strand of her long, straightened hair behind her ear and offered a smile at Anissa's annoyed face.

"What do you want?" Anissa asked.

"I just came to see if you wanted to head out with us. Leon is letting us go shopping for a few hours."

"And if I say no?"

"Then none of us can go. He said you have to hold the money he's giving us."

"Why can't he just take y'all then?"

"Because he has somewhere important to be. So pleee-ase? Say you'll come. The only time I've been out of this house in the past two weeks was to sell some pussy. I'm tired of seeing walls. I need some fresh air!"

"I had plans today," Anissa lied through her teeth.

"To go see your cousin in the hospital?" Harmony guessed.

All Anissa wanted was to lie in bed all day and watch movies, but the reason she didn't have the will to do anything was because her thoughts went back to Brynn. All Harmony's question did was remind her of that. It also reminded her that she hadn't been to the hospital since that first night to visit, mainly because she felt ashamed that she was still angry at her cousin. And that anger made her feel guilt. She couldn't go near Brynn with those feelings of contempt while she was in the situation she was in.

"No," Anissa answered. "Plus, I know she has cops sniffing all around her because somebody tried to kill her. Probably one of her crazy-ass tricks."

"I still think you should go see her. Just ask daddy. He might let you go. He might even want to come with you," she said and averted her eyes quickly.

"It's none of your business. Y'all are nosy as hell around this house," Anissa said.

"That's what happens when all you have is each other. There aren't any secrets. So please, if whatever you have to do isn't important, please come."

"Fine. Let me get ready," Anissa groaned and tossed her covers to the side.

Harmony did a little jump and clapped her hands in excitement before she left. Anissa assumed that she was going to tell the others the good news. She wondered why Leon didn't want to give them the money. The way he had them on lock, she was sure that they wouldn't try to run away. It took her about thirty minutes to get ready, and when she went down to the kitchen, everyone was there waiting for her, including Leon. He was wearing a suit and had a pair of Stacy Adams on his feet. She couldn't see his eyes because of the dark shades over them, but she could tell that he was staring her down when she entered the kitchen.

"I have five racks for my girls to blow today. Make sure they get something nice," Leon said and handed her one envelope of money. "And this is another three racks just for you."

He handed her a second envelope filled with money. Anissa took notice of CoCo slightly rolling her eyes in the background, and even the other two girls looked a little annoyed, but nobody said anything. She took the money and put it in her new Chanel bag with a nod.

"I want them back in the house before five. They have a long work night ahead of them. Take your car. And no funny business. I'll know where you are."

"You say that like you have a tracker on my car," Anissa said, half joking, but the look Leon gave her made her grow serious. "You put a tracker on my car?"

"I have to know where my merchandise is at all times. I do it for your safety. I told you, I have membership meetings at the Fantasy Factory, queen. We'll be open before you know it, and the real money will start rolling in. I want to make sure you are all safe until then."

Anissa wanted to say some more about him tracking them, but Harmony shot her a look that told her to think again. She bit the inside of her cheek and found a different set of words to speak.

"I hope so, because if I don't start making my own money soon, our little arrangement here will be null and void."

Anissa was speaking on the fact that she'd promised not to go out and make her own money by herself. She still had a little stacked, but she hadn't been able to add to it. She hadn't realized it at the time, but opening the Groove Boutique had dug deeper into her stash than she had thought. Back then, Anissa didn't think anything of it, because in her mind she was going to be able to make it back. However, the turn of events proved otherwise. She wouldn't tell Leon, but she was counting on the money he'd promised her that she would make with him, and so far, he had turned up with nothing but gifts. She was depending on the Fantasy Factory to be as successful as he thought it was going to be.

"Don't fret, queen. I told you I got you."

"I hope so," Anissa said and gave him a wink before turning to the girls. "All right, bitches, let's go since y'all done dragged me out of bed. And if one of them long, pointy-ass nails y'all have scratches my leather, I'm beating ass."

When they left, the first place the girls headed to was, of course, the mall. It was the first time Anissa had ever been alone with the girls, and she could literally feel the newfound ease in the atmosphere. When Leon was around, they didn't talk unless spoken to. But there in her car, they were complete chatterboxes.

"I need to get some new nude open-toe shoes! The ones I have now are disgusting!" Harmony was saying. "The last muthafucka I wore them for was into some kinky shit. He made me put my heel in his ass."

"Bitch, that doesn't even take the cake. Some of the shit these men have had me do hasn't even been written about yet," CoCo told her from the front passenger seat. "That's why men love paying for pussy. They can let all their nasty fetishes out and know you're just gonna take it."

"Y'all don't charge extra for shit like that?" Anissa inquired.

"We don't set the prices. Daddy does. And he tells us to make sure they have a good time, no matter what."

"Well, that's the problem right there." Anissa shook her head. "You only become a ho when you let a man treat you like one. And if y'all are doing all that for fifteen hundred dollars, that's ho shit."

"Well, excuse me, but not all of us can be five thousand a pop," CoCo commented.

"And why not?" Anissa said, making a face at CoCo. "When I got to South Beach, I had never escorted a day in my life. But on my very first date I made three thousand dollars. Why? Because no matter what, I carry myself like a lady. I never acted thirsty for money, so my clients were more willing to give it to me. I set my own rules, and they followed them if they wanted any piece of me. Also, it's important to have regular clients. A regular customer knows and is used to paying your fee. They know what to expect, and you build a regular rapport with them. They trust you, and because of that, you learn to trust them. I've never needed a pimp because I followed those rules. I also keep a gun in my purse."

"Daddy won't let us have guns," Angel told her.

"Because he owns you, that's why," Anissa responded.

The car got quiet. The only sound was the wind blowing through the cracked windows. Anissa felt that maybe she had gone a little too far with her comment, but it was the truth. Leon owned them, and he was trying to own her. She wasn't stupid. He wasn't fooling anybody with the whole "queen" thing. She would bet all the money left in her savings that every girl in that car had been his "queen" at one point or another.

"Anissa?"

"What's up?" she asked and glanced in the rearview at Harmony.

"Will you teach us everything you know?"

"That's what I told Leon I would do."

"No, I mean . . . how to work for ourselves."

"Harmony!" CoCo exclaimed from the front seat, whipping around and giving Harmony a crazed look. "What you saying, girl? Daddy would kill you if he knew you asked something like that."

"Like the way he almost killed you when you asked him for more of the money you earned?"

"I was tripping that night. We all know daddy is supposed to keep all the money. We work for him. It was kind of him to give us the two hundred dollars. Right, Angel?"

"Two hundred dollars?" Anissa interrupted, then laughed, because it had to be a joke. But from the looks on their faces, it wasn't. "He only gives you two hundred dollars out of all the money you make?"

She didn't know why she was as shocked as she was. For one, she'd read somewhere that a pimp kept the majority of all earnings from their hoes. Also, he wouldn't even let them touch their own shopping money, which was technically their money anyway. No wonder he was able to live so good. With the checks from the farm, plus the girls bringing in thousands every night, Leon was living the life. Suddenly it worried her if he would even keep his end of the bargain.

"Daddy takes care of us," CoCo told her simply. "He buys us everything we need and keeps a roof over our heads. What do we really need money for?"

"To travel and to experience life," Anissa said, throwing out a few suggestions.

"We aren't allowed to go anywhere without daddy. He pays for everything."

"And you're okay with that?" Anissa asked.

CoCo shrugged her shoulders and went back to forward facing. Her eyes were straight ahead, but Anissa could tell that it wasn't the road she was seeing. Her jaw was tensed, and her eyes had glossed over like she was lost in a thought.

"How did you start working for Leon, CoCo? Angel told me her story. But I don't know yours."

"I don't want to talk about it," CoCo told her. "Especially not to the bitch trying to take my spot as lead girl."

"Take your spot?" Anissa asked. "I'm just trying to get some money, just like you. Leon put an offer on the table, so now I'm here."

"The only reason I've been so nice to you is because daddy told us to. You think I don't see right through what you're doing? With all that back talk to daddy that you're doing?" CoCo turned to Anissa and mugged her. "You're trying to be his bottom bitch, aren't you? Well, I got news for you. That position is already filled. And I don't want to be like you. I don't want to learn how to walk and talk like you. I've been here the longest out of all of us bitches, and I've done things, things that you can't even imagine, to keep my daddy's pockets full. I'm loyal! He loves me. I don't care how many times you fuck him. I'm gonna be the one here in the end. I'm gonna make him so proud at the Fantasy Factory."

"Well, news flash, I haven't fucked the nigga and don't plan to," Anissa told her.

"Daddy always tries out his product before he puts it on the market," Angel said from the back seat. "If he hasn't had you yet, he will before he opens the Fantasy Factory. Daddy always gets his way."

"Maybe with you brainless bitches. The first thing I'm gonna teach you is how to think for yourself. You can't walk or talk like me if you don't. Oh, wait, I forgot CoCo doesn't want that. She wants to be Leon's bottom bitch on her own," Anissa scoffed. "What happened in your life that was that terrible to make you aspire to be someone's property?"

"I told you I don't want to talk about it," CoCo said.

"It's okay, CoCo. We aren't in daddy's car. He can't hear us talking," Angel said.

"He can't hear us talking? What does that mean?"

"Daddy has the whole house bugged. His cars, too. It's his way of making sure we aren't talking about things we shouldn't be talking about."

"Like right now. Y'all are gonna make daddy hurt me again. I keep being disobedient, and he doesn't like that. My eye just healed," CoCo said, pulling the visor down and looking into her pretty face.

That would have been the perfect time to drop them off and keep it moving with her life, but it only made Anissa more curious. Angel had already told her about how she'd gotten to where she was now, but Harmony's and CoCo's histories were a mystery.

When they finally got to the mall, CoCo and Angel ran inside Victoria's Secret, but Harmony hung back. She took a seat on the bench outside the store and waited for them to get done. She was watching all the people hustling and bustling around the place, and when Anissa sat next to her, she saw a longing in Harmony's eyes.

"You good?"

"I don't know the last time I went somewhere without daddy breathing down my neck," Harmony answered.

"So, what you said back in the car, about you wanting to learn how to work for yourself, you were serious?"

"I . . . I don't know." She shrugged. "Daddy will never let me go. He tells us if we try to leave, he'll kill us. And I believe him."

"Have you ever tried?" Anissa asked, and Harmony shook her head. "Well, since CoCo won't tell me, how did you end up here, Harmony? Caught up with Leon, I mean."

"I met Leon a little while after I was gang raped at a party when I was in college at TSU," Harmony told her without batting an eye. "They did things to me that no woman should have done to her. They recorded it and posted it for the whole school to see. I pressed charges."

"So, they went to jail?"

"Nope." Harmony shook her head with a scoff. "One of the guy's dads was a lawyer, a good one. He represented all of them, and they got off scot-free. I couldn't go back to school. I was broken. So, I dropped out and got addicted to painkillers."

"What about your family? They didn't try to help you?"

"My parents told me that the whole thing was my fault. That maybe if I hadn't dressed so provocatively, none of it would have happened. All they wanted was for me to enroll back in school, but I couldn't. I couldn't face the people who had defiled my body. Nobody cared that most days I didn't even feel like a human being. The drugs were the only thing keeping me afloat. But then they took those away from me, and the withdrawal gave me terrible nightmares about what happened. I couldn't stay there anymore, so I bought a bus pass and came here to Florida with two hundred dollars to my name. No one would hire me, so I did the only thing I could think of. I became a prostitute."

"That's how you met Leon?"

"Yeah." She nodded. "I was meeting up with a dude at this rinky-dink hotel, and what I didn't know was that he never planned to pay me. In fact, he and a few of his friends thought they were gonna have a good ol' free time."

"You got gang raped again?"

"Almost, but no. Leon and CoCo were coincidently at the same hotel at the time. He heard me screaming and stopped it before it happened. He beat them up bad."

"He saved you," Anissa noted, understanding Harmony's loyalty.

"Yeah, and he took me home with him that night. He told me I could stay with him as long as I liked. He didn't have to tell me what he was. One look at Angel and CoCo and I knew. But I didn't care. Daddy is so charming he could woo the feathers off a bird. He called me queen back then too, ya know? We did things that couples do, even made love. He was good to me, bought me anything I wanted without asking. He treated me like royalty. Until . . ."

"Until he didn't." Anissa shook her head.

"I wanted to pay him back for all the nice things he'd done for me. And since I was already hooking, I thought, why not work with CoCo and Angel? But once I did, everything changed. The first time he slapped me was because I didn't make his toast right. Split my lip down the middle. The next time, he broke my jaw because I didn't wash his clothes right. At first, I told myself to leave. That I didn't deserve that, but then I realized it was my fault for making daddy angry. Because after he hurt me, he would make me feel good. He would do nice things for me."

"He would break you down so that he could build you up again," Anissa said. "Classic behavior of an abuser. He did that to control you, Harmony. You don't deserve that."

"It doesn't matter what I deserve. I'm his property. I get whatever he thinks I deserve. He made us all think we were special. We all thought we were gonna be his bottom bitch, but the truth is, no one is. We're all the same. The moment you sell yourself for him is the second he'll change and become his true self to you. But you . . . he does treat you differently. Like he treated . . ." Harmony stopped talking mid-sentence and had an expression like she'd said too much.

"Like he treated who?" Anissa raised her brow. "Like he treated who, Harmony?"

"I can't talk about it. Excuse me." Harmony stood up and hurried inside of Victoria's Secret.

Her actions were very strange, and Anissa wanted to know why. She clenched her jaw. Maybe she had made a mistake agreeing to work for Leon. Not all money was good money. She was so fixed on her thoughts of Leon, Harmony, CoCo, and Angel that she hadn't seen someone walking up on her.

"Anissa?" a voice asked.

She looked up from where she sat and saw a handsome man holding a few shopping bags standing over her. It was Kendall, the guy who had told her to take his number at Loelle's weeks ago. So much had happened since then that she'd never used it.

"Kendall, hey," she said. The smile on her face came naturally because even though she didn't know him at all, it was good to see a familiar face. He was even finer than she remembered, and it might have had something to do with the fresh cut he was sporting. Not to mention, he was looking quite nice in his gray joggers. It was taking everything in her not to stare at the bulge protruding from them.

"I didn't know if I would ever see you again. I was sure you would use my number, but maybe I wasn't as charming as I thought."

"Oh, no, trust me, you were. A lot has happened since then. I just kind of forgot about you."

"Damn, that was blunt," he said, making a hissing sound with his tongue like he'd just gotten burned.

"No! I didn't mean it like that. I'm sorry." Anissa could have smacked herself. "My cousin got hurt, and some things happened with our business. I've just been trying to process a lot, that's all."

"Oh, I'm sorry to hear about your cousin," he said sincerely and sat down next to her. "Is she all right?"

"She got shot and has been in a coma since."

"Damn."

"She's alive though, so that has to matter somewhere, right?"

"Yeah, gotta count your blessings as they come. But that's still fucked up. Is there anything I can do?"

"No, it's okay."

"Nah, for real. Maybe I can take you out sometime and get your mind off everything. What about this weekend?"

"Umm . . ." Anissa wanted to say yes so badly. But her words were thwarted when she saw CoCo staring intently from inside the store at the two of them talking. "Can I let you know? I can text you and tell you if I'm free."

"Are you gonna use my number for real this time?"

"I promise," she told him.

"I'ma hold you to that." He took her hand in his and rubbed it gently before kissing her knuckles with his soft lips.

Had it really been that long since she'd been touched by a man? Because her clit throbbed and wanted him to press the monster he was working with against it. When he left, she watched him walk away and took note of his cute butt until he disappeared into the crowd.

"Anissa, we're ready to check out!" she heard Angel call from the store, and Anissa suddenly remembered she had the money on her.

"Here I come!"

When she went into the store to pay for the lingerie they'd picked out, she avoided CoCo's condescending stare. The transaction came to just over $1,000, and Anissa handed the clerk the bills. The right side of her face was burning from the laser beams it felt like CoCo was sending with her eyes, and Anissa couldn't get out of that store fast enough. Only, CoCo had to come with her. They decided they were going to look at shoes next, but that time Angel and Harmony went ahead while CoCo hung back.

"Who was that?" she asked Anissa.

"Who was who?"

"That nigga you were talking to."

"None of your business," Anissa said, making a face. She tried to go into the shoe store with the others, but CoCo grabbed her arm forcefully and held her back.

"Any disrespect to daddy is my business."

"I know you better get your fucking hand off me before I break it."

"I will when you tell me who that was you were giving googly eyes to. Daddy doesn't like us to flirt. Especially since we're out spending his money."

"Bitch, I don't know what you don't understand about the fact that I'm not like you or either of them." Anissa pointed to where Angel and Harmony were. "I don't belong to anybody. I'ma talk to whoever the fuck I want to talk to. I can do whatever I want. Leon was sniffing around my coattails like a lost puppy, not the other way around. I'm not one of his 'Delights.' Right now, that nigga ain't shit to me but a place to rest my head, but if everything isn't everything with this gentlemen's club, I'm out."

When she was done talking, CoCo just stared at her for a few seconds. Then she began laughing. Anissa didn't understand what was so funny and wanted to snatch the high ponytail out of CoCo's head. CoCo let her arm go and shook her head.

"You sound just like her."

"Like who?"

"Bubbles."

"Who is Bubbles?" Anissa asked.

"The last girl who thought she was above daddy's laws."

"What happened to her?"

"Keep disrespecting daddy and you'll find out. He always gives new girls passes. He likes to make you think you have a choice. But the truth is that you don't. You gave that right up the moment you walked through his doors. So, my advice to you, Anissa, would be to tread lightly. You have daddy's attention now, and that means he will never let you go. You can keep fooling yourself with this high and mighty act all you want. But in the end, we all get broken down."

CoCo left Anissa standing in the hallway by herself. The hairs on the back of her neck were standing up as CoCo's words played over and over in her head. *Had* she been fooling herself? The truth was that ever since she met Leon, she'd never felt free of him. And what about the other girl, Bubbles? Who was she? Leon had never made mention of her, and Anissa was going to find out why.

Chapter 13

When they got back to the house, Leon was still gone. But it was only a few hours before five o'clock, and she knew that he could come back at any time. Anissa wanted to get Harmony alone again, away from CoCo, who seemed to be the most loyal. So, she waited to leave her room until Harmony, CoCo, and Angel were in their rooms getting ready for their night of work. She crept down the hallway, careful not to make too much noise when she passed CoCo's door, and knocked on Harmony's door.

"I told you, they didn't put your panties in my bag." Harmony popped her head out when she opened the door, but then she saw it was Anissa. "Oh, I thought you were Angel. That bitch keeps saying the lady at Victoria's Secret put her thong with my stuff."

"Can I come in?"

"Sure, I was just about to hop in the shower."

Harmony opened the door all the way, revealing herself wearing only a bra and panties. She stepped out of the way so that Anissa could step in, and when Anissa did, she shut the door behind her. She tried to think of how she wanted to start her questions, but no words found her tongue. Harmony noticed the way that she was staring at her and widened her eyes.

"Umm, daddy doesn't like for us to sleep together. Only if he's there too," she said, throwing Anissa off.

"What?" she asked, and then she understood what Harmony meant. She shook her head. "Oh! That's not what I'm here for. You're fine and all, but I don't eat pussy for any price. I'm here because I want to ask you something about what we talked about earlier. About the girl who isn't here anymore."

"Shhh!" Harmony said quickly and pressed a finger to her lips. A look of fear overcame her, and she looked frantically around the room, even though they were the only ones there.

"Harmony, did something happen to her?"

"Shhh! Somebody might hear you," Harmony said in a low voice. "I can't talk about that."

"Why?"

"Because we aren't supposed to!"

"Please just tell me what happened to her. CoCo made it seem like it was something bad. And if I'm here now, I should know."

Harmony still looked like she didn't want to say anything. But after a few moments of Anissa pleading her down with her eyes, Harmony finally grabbed Anissa's hand and took her into the bathroom. Once there, she shut the door and turned the shower and the sink faucet on.

"We don't know where he has the house bugged," Harmony whispered. "But we know he does. He beat Angel so bad for talking about leaving a year ago. He hadn't been home when she said it, but he repeated everything like he was. I have to be careful."

"Okay," Anissa whispered back. "Who is Bubbles?"

"Was."

"Was?"

"Who *was* Bubbles."

"What does that mean, Harmony?"

"Bubbles was the girl after me," Harmony sighed. "She was young and a firecracker at the mouth, just like you. And also like you, she had been working for herself. Making her own money in the streets without a pimp. But she let Leon talk her into working for him. He brought her home earlier this year and told us she was going to be the main attraction of something big he had planned."

"The Fantasy Factory."

"We know that now, but back then he wouldn't tell us. We thought he was just talking. But in the meantime, she made him a lot of money. She was black and Asian, so men went crazy over her. They were calling for dates with her every night, so much that he sometimes would have to offer us other girls for half price when she wasn't available."

"So, what happened? If she was making him so much money, I mean."

"He wasn't giving her any of it even though he said he would. She didn't like that, and when she tried to leave . . . things got ugly."

"This bitch must have stolen my flat iron again!" Harmony growled as she rummaged around underneath her sink trying to find it. "Daddy bought her one of her own!"

All she wanted to do was iron her new wig to wear that night with her skintight red minidress. Leon told them they were meeting some very important people that night, and all Harmony wanted to do was look her best. They'd been making Leon so much money, and he'd been very happy lately, so happy that he was constantly showering them with gifts, and Harmony couldn't remember the last time he'd hit any of his girls.

Harmony stormed out of her room and tried to get her attitude together as she made her way to CoCo's room. She was getting tired of CoCo going through her

personal things. There was a reason why Leon had al-
lowed them to all have their own rooms, and Harmony
was constantly reminding her of that. On her way,
Harmony passed the new girl's room and noticed that
the door was slightly ajar. She turned her head and
peeked inside as she passed, and what she saw made her
stop in her tracks. Bubbles had been with them for a little
over a month and was the reason Leon had been in such
a good mood. All his girls were beautiful, but Bubbles
had a look that none of them had. She was mixed race,
which meant she was a black girl with Asian features.
Her cheekbones were sharp, and her wide, pretty brown
eyes were slanted. She had perky breasts, a small waist,
and wide hips. Her plump ass was just the icing on the
cake. Bubbles had brought Leon and the other girls a
lot of business, which was why Harmony was shocked
to see her packing her bags in a hurry. She was so fo-
cused on stuffing them with as much as would fit that
she didn't hear Harmony push the door open.

"Going somewhere?" Harmony asked, making Bubbles
jump.

Bubbles whisked around with wide, fearful eyes.
When she saw that it was Harmony and not Leon, she
relaxed slightly, but not much. She turned back to her
bags and zipped both of them up before heading over to
her dresser and sliding her jewelry into her purse.

Harmony tried again when she didn't get an answer
to her first question. "Bubbles, is everything okay?
You're wearing all black and packing your bags like
you're about to leave."

"I have to get out of here," Bubbles said in a hurry.

"But why? Aren't you happy with us?"

"I thought . . . I thought I would be able to make good
money with Leon. But he doesn't give me any of it."

"What do you need money for when daddy gives us everything we need?" When she said it, even Harmony had to admit that she sounded like a robot. Like what she had said had been programmed to come out of her mouth.

Bubbles looked at Harmony with disbelief. "And the sad thing is that you really believe that," she scoffed. "He lied to me. He told me that if I came here for six months and worked with him, I could leave with half of what I earned. He hasn't given me a penny, and he won't let me leave. He took away my cell phone, and he sold my car. If he even thinks I'm thinking about leaving, he beats me. I can't do it anymore. I told my ex-boyfriend that Leon would be gone tonight, and he's on his way to get me now."

"We've all tried to leave before. He always finds us. And each time he does, the punishment is . . ." Harmony shuddered, thinking about the first and only time she tried to get away from Leon. When he found her, he brought her back to the house and beat her so badly that she couldn't walk. Afterward, he tied her up in her room for a week without food or water. She was sitting in her own pee and feces, inhaling her own stench for days before he came to check on her. He told her that since she was still alive, he would forgive her. But if she ever tried to get away from him again, she wouldn't be alive to regret it. He told her that she was his forever.

"Well, I have to try. He won't find me if I'm in another state far away from here. There is something really, really wrong with Leon. He's a devil."

"I know," Harmony whispered.

"If you know, then why are you still here?" Bubbles asked and stared intently into Harmony's eyes.

The simplest answer was that Harmony had nowhere to go. Even if she had gotten away the first time, she had *no one. Her parents were dead, and she was an only child. She didn't know her other family, and since she never graduated high school or obtained a GED, there was no place she could get a job. Leon gave her all the things she couldn't get herself. But as the years passed, Harmony was starting to feel the burden of her soul contract. The distress and fear written all over Bubble's face were familiar to Harmony because they came with belonging to Leon. Every move she made was done to please him, even when he wasn't around. It wasn't until she stood there staring at someone bold enough to try to get away that she realized she wanted to try again too. She would rather have her freedom and nothing else than the false sense of security that Leon provided.*

"Bubbles—" Harmony started.

"Don't try to talk me out of it."

"Take me with you," Harmony finished in a whisper.

"What?" Bubbles was visibly shocked. "'I thought 'daddy gives us everything we need.'"

"He does. He gives us everything but the one thing that matters. Freedom. I don't know who I am anymore. But I do know that I want to find her. And I also know that if you leave, Leon is gonna go back to beating us like dogs again. I can't go back to that. I won't."

Bubbles studied Harmony, trying to see if she was serious. And she was.

"Okay. Go grab whatever you can in five minutes. He said he'll be here tonight at nine thirty on the dot when I called him last night at the party we did. I used one of my trick's phones after he passed out."

"Okay," Harmony said.

"And don't say anything to the others. I don't trust CoCo. I barely trust you. The moment we're far enough away, you're getting dropped off and you're on your own."

Harmony nodded and hurried out of the room. The flat iron was the last thing on her mind when she was back in the hallway. She looked toward CoCo's and Angel's doors to make sure they hadn't heard any of what had just transpired, but they were still closed. She assumed that they were getting ready for the night, and if that was the case, they wouldn't show their faces until it was time to leave.

Once back in her room, Harmony snatched two empty Louis Vuitton duffle bags down from her closet. Leon had bought them for her to use when they all went out of town for parties, but that night they would be used to get away from him. Far away. If she could have seen the future when she had first come to stay with Leon, she would have rather struggled on the streets. Some days, Harmony forgot she was a person. Most days she just felt like nothing. Like her existence didn't matter. But she wanted it to. She wanted to matter to somebody. And to Leon, all she would ever be was a pussy in a dress.

She stuffed the bags with as much as she could and forced the zippers closed. After that, she changed out of the slip she was wearing to throw on a pair of jeans and a hoodie. When her shoes were on, she went back into the hallway and saw that Bubbles was already running to the stairs with her own bags in tow.

"Come on!" Bubbles urged in a whisper. "I'm sure he's outside already."

"Okay!" Harmony said, but when she took two steps, the strap of one of her bags snapped. It was too heavy. "Wait!"

Bubbles looked back at Harmony and saw her struggling with the bag. She hesitated, but not for long.

"I can't," Bubbles said, shaking her head. "I have to leave. I have to get out of here!"

"Don't leave me!"

But Bubbles either didn't hear her or didn't care. She rushed down the staircase like there was fire on her heels. Harmony tried to pick the bag up but fumbled it. She decided to just leave it and tried to hightail it to the top of the stairs. By the time she got halfway down them, she saw that Bubbles was already at the front door. Bubbles had her hand out to turn the knob when the heavy door flew open, like someone had pushed it forcefully.

"Hey, man! I told you I had the wrong address!" a man exclaimed as he stumbled into the house.

He whipped around and put his hands up with a fear-stricken expression. Harmony didn't recognize him, but she recognized the person behind him. Leon stepped inside of his home with a look of contempt written all over his face. In his hands, there was a pistol pointed right at the man's chest. Before she could be seen, Harmony hurried back up the steps out of sight, but to where she could still peek over the wall and see what was going on. Her legs were shaking, but she tried her best to stay silent and still.

Bubbles was frozen where she stood, and her chest heaved up and down in terror. Leon let the door shut behind him, and his eyes went from the man to Bubbles, and then to the bags she was carrying. His gun stayed directed at the man, but his words were directed at her.

"Care to tell me where you're going?"

"I . . . I was just bringing my things down here for the party later. So I wouldn't have to carry them downstairs in my heels."

"Then why is he here?"

"I don't know. I've never seen him before in my life," Bubbles told him.

"Take a good look at him. Are you sure you don't know him? Because he looks a lot like that ex-boyfriend of yours."

"What?"

"Don't play stupid with me!" daddy bellowed. "Do you think I would ever bring you into my house without looking into your past, Bubbles? Do you think I don't know Keith when I see him?"

Bubbles' eyes widened, and she realized that she'd been caught. Her hands tightened around her bag, and her eyes darted to the door behind Leon.

"Hey, man. She just told me she needed a ride. I didn't—"

"Shut up!" Leon silenced him by smacking him across the face with his gun.

Harmony pressed her hands tightly against her mouth to muffle her gasp when she saw the blood fly. Keith fell to the ground, clutching his face. A bloody gash had formed underneath his left eye.

"You tryin'a leave me?" Leon asked and jerked the gun toward Keith. "With him? Don't you know I own you, bitch?"

"Nobody owns me! I'm not staying here! And you can't make me!" Bubbles screamed at him.

"You know what?" Leon said and laughed like something was funny. "You are one ungrateful bitch, you know that? I give you everything! Everything any other female would kill to have. And you want to throw it in my face."

"You give me those things with the money I make. You just take it! I can't do it anymore. I was doing fine without you before. I'll be fine without you again. Come on, Keith, let's go."

Bubbles went to help Keith up, but the sound of Leon's gun cocking stopped her. She looked back to him and saw that he now had the gun pointed at her.

"I'm afraid I can't let you do that, shawty. You belong to me forever now."

"*There is something seriously wrong with you. You think you're a pimp, but you're really just a man who can't get anybody to really love your weird ass. Because you're a monster. Probably overcompensating for your daddy issues.*"

"*You know, you're right about the daddy part,*" Leon agreed. "*My old man wasn't much of a dad. That's why I killed him.*"

"*You what?*"

"*I killed him, not the cancer. He fell ill and went to the hospital. He probably would have made a full recovery if I weren't overdosing him through the IV.*" He laughed. "*The nurses thought it was their fault.*"

"*You really are a monster.*" Bubbles shook her head.

"*After I'm done with your punishment, you'll never call me anything but 'daddy' ever again.*"

"*I'll die before I stay here or call you that,*" Bubbles spat.

"*Man, she can stay. My car is running. I just wanna go home,*" Keith said with wide eyes.

"*You should have thought about that before you came to my spot tryin'a steal my property.*"

Boom!

The sound of the gun was deafening, which was a good thing because that time Harmony wasn't able to muffle her cry. Leon had shot Keith right through the neck, but he didn't die right away. Keith's hands clutched the spot where the blood was gushing out as he fell to his side. He choked on his own blood for a good thirty seconds before finally his body went limp. Bubbles had her mouth open in a silent scream as the scene unfolded before her. Tears streamed down her face, and she took a few steps away from Leon.

"*How could you? You killed him!*"

"No, you killed him," Leon told her. "You're the reason he has a bullet lodged in his throat, not me. I just came home to make sure you bitches were ready to go, and I find you tryin'a run away from me. After all I've done for you?"

"The only thing you've done for me is take my freedom. Fuck you. I'm going to the cops about Keith."

"Is that right?" Leon asked in a tone so frigid that even Harmony felt chills down her spine. He took a step toward Bubbles, and she took another step back. "How you gon' do that if you're dead?"

Right before Leon pounced on her, Bubbles glanced up at the place Harmony was watching from. Their eyes were locked on each other when Leon wrapped his hands around her neck and forced her to the ground.

"I had high hopes for you," Leon said breathily as Bubbles struggled under him, but no matter what she did, she couldn't evade his clutches. "But you know what they say about a bitch you can't train. You gotta put her down."

Bubbles choked and tried to claw at his hands, but she grew weaker and weaker by the moment. When her arms fell to her sides, Leon jerked her one more time before letting her go. Harmony could tell by the emptiness in her eyes that she was dead. Leon must have seen Bubbles glance Harmony's way, because when he stood up, he whipped his head in the same direction. She ducked quickly and held her breath. She had to get back to her room. If he found her there with her bags packed, he would surely kill her too.

Harmony placed one duffle bag on her shoulder and ran to grab the broken bag, placing it under her other arm. She hurried back to her room, trying to keep her footsteps as quiet as possible. She didn't know if Leon had begun making his way up the stairs yet. She also *didn't know if Angel and CoCo had heard the gunshot in the big house. If either of them caught her in the hallway, they would for sure tell Leon what she had been up to.*

Harmony made it to her bedroom just as she heard Leon's footsteps coming up the top of the staircase. She closed her door and, thinking on her toes, rushed to stash her bags in the bathroom tub. She closed the shower curtains and frantically took off her shoes and clothes to throw deep into her closet. She was going back to the bathroom in her underwear to finish getting ready for the night when her bedroom door swung open.

Leon stood in the doorway with a blaze in his eyes as he surveyed her room like he was looking for something out of place. When finally they landed on her half-naked body, they traveled up to her chest and stayed there. He watched as she breathed, and when his eyes met hers, she felt the heat coming from them.

"Why are you breathing so heavily?" he asked suspiciously.

"I was running," she answered truthfully.

He nodded his head and entered her room. He didn't stop walking until their bodies almost touched and he was towering above her. She lowered her head, not wanting to look into his eyes anymore, but he lifted her chin forcefully.

"Why were you running?"

"I . . . I—"

"If you're thinking about lying to me, I would think wisely about that, baby girl. You of all people know what happens when someone does something I don't like. Were you in the hallway?"

"I . . ." Harmony swallowed the air that was stuck in her throat. "Yes. I was in the hallway, daddy."

"Why?"

"CoCo stole my flat iron again. I was going to get it back, and then . . ."

"And then what?"

"I heard your voice, and then I heard a gunshot. So, I ran back to my room," Harmony lied, trying to keep her expression still.

Leon always knew when she was lying. But she couldn't reveal that she'd witnessed the whole thing: him murdering both Keith and Bubbles, or the fact that she'd heard him confess to killing his father. She might not have been the brightest crayon in the box, but she knew that the only good place for someone knowing your worst deeds was a box in the ground.

"You heard a gunshot and you didn't come see what happened?"

"No. A good ho knows her place," she told him, shaking her head.

Her bottom lip trembled at the mercy of his vivid stare. He didn't believe her. She just knew it. In seconds he would search her room and find the bags she had packed. She didn't want that to happen. She wasn't ready to die. Her eyes lowered again and fell on a few droplets of blood on his dress shirt.

"Daddy." She feigned worry. "You have blood on your shirt. Are you hurt? Did somebody break in? Is that why I heard a gunshot?"

She pretended to care by running her hands over him as if to check for injuries. She only hoped her acting was good enough for him to believe that she truly hadn't seen what had happened. He grabbed her hands, forcing them to stop moving, and stepped away from her. The next time she looked into his eyes, the fire in them was slightly extinguished. He shook his head at her and sighed.

"I have bad news. Bubbles is no longer one of Leon's Delights."

"What?" Harmony made her eyes grow wide.

"I caught her tryin'a run up out of here with my money to be with one of her tricks," Leon lied through his teeth. "They tried to get at me, and I had to handle my business. You understand that, don't you? Why I had to kill them?"

Harmony slowly nodded her head. But it was then that she realized that she hadn't just been living with a man who sometimes punished them cruelly to keep them in their place. She had been living with a cold-blooded killer. He leaned forward and placed a kiss on her forehead.

"Good. Because I need you to get the other girls to go in the back and start digging. We have to get rid of the bodies."

By the time Harmony was done with the story, Anissa's blood pressure had risen to an unhealthy level. She knew the story was true by how visibly shaken Harmony was. She had tears running down her face, and Anissa could only imagine how she felt. She now understood why the girls were so obedient. They knew Leon would really murder them because they'd seen his bodies firsthand. And what about her? There she was, thinking that she would be able to leave whenever she wanted, but Harmony's story proved otherwise. Leon would never let her go. In her, he'd found the moneymaker he'd lost in Bubbles.

"Oh, my God," she whispered and sat down on the toilet.

"And, Anissa, that's not all," Harmony whispered and grabbed her hands. "There's more."

"What else could there be?" Anissa breathed. "He made you guys hide more bodies?"

"No." Harmony shook her head. "This is about the night your cousin was shot."

"What about that night?" Anissa asked and felt her hands tighten around Harmony's.

"I don't know the complete details, but I know that same night, daddy came home later than usual. I was in the kitchen, but he didn't know I was there, and I heard him mumbling to himself."

"What was he saying?"

"He said . . . I heard him say that he should have shot her in the head and made sure that she was dead. But now he has you right where he wants you. He said now he finally has his star girl."

"Me?" Anissa asked. Harmony nodded. "Are you telling me that Leon tried to murder my cousin? So, I'd come and work for him?"

"I believe so." Harmony nodded. "And now that he has you, there is no way out."

Anissa gently pulled her hands away and tried to process what Harmony had just said. Her eyes were on the marble floor of the bathroom as her thoughts went a thousand miles a minute. She had so many emotions coursing through her: anger at what Leon had done to Brynn, and regret because she was the one who had brought him into their lives. Anissa knew that for now Brynn was safe from him because of the murder investigation. Her room was being watched due to the active murder investigation. Still, now that Anissa knew who had been behind it, she wasn't sure how long Brynn would be safe. Not if she could identify Leon as the shooter when she finally regained consciousness. Anissa wouldn't let Leon get another crack at hurting her. Not only that, but she refused to be a pawn in his gentlemen's club. He had to go down. But how? How could she get away from him without ending up like Bubbles? Suddenly, Anissa remembered she wasn't the only one who wanted to get away from Leon. And just like that, she had an idea. Heart thumping, she looked back up into Harmony's eyes.

"Harmony. Are the bodies of Bubbles and Keith still in the backyard?"

"No." Harmony shook her head, putting an instant halt on Anissa's plans. "That night he made us think we were digging graves, but really he was just buying himself time to get rid of the bodies himself. By the time we were done digging, Keith and Bubbles were gone. He told us he had no choice but to trust us with his secret, but he would never trust us with the proof. Shortly after that, he bugged the house. He wanted to know what we were talking about at all times."

"Damn!" Anissa exclaimed. "There has to be another way."

They grew silent for a while, and Anissa watched the water running down the drain. She thought about just running away, but then she remembered Leon could track her location. She wouldn't get very far on foot. Not even to the interstate to hitchhike. When the feeling of defeat began to wash over her, Harmony gasped.

"Your cousin!" she said.

"What about her?"

"She didn't die! Which means daddy has unfinished business with her. He's not gonna want to go to prison for attempted murder if he has one of the biggest businesses in the city about to open up. He's gonna try to finish the job. We have to catch him in the act."

"I'm not about to put Brynn in the line of fire again. Not like that. Not with him," Anissa told her.

"She won't be in the line of fire if the police are there to catch him."

Anissa finally understood what she was saying. She tried to think of another way, but that was the best idea, and she knew it. After a few seconds, she nodded her head in agreement.

"We have to set him up."

Chapter 14

Leon sat in what would be his office once the Fantasy Factory was open for business in two weeks. He'd been able to push up the opening date because he'd gotten enough people to sign up and pledge their membership loyalty. He'd also scouted the best-fitting girls from local strip joints and added more eye candy to his lineup since his girls had failed in that department. For now, his Delights would be the only ones to service those with white card status, and the others would have to earn their keep. Plus, the fewer girls to service his most lucrative clients, the more exclusive they would be.

His office was almost complete. Leon figured it would only be fitting to have a royal theme. His club-footed desk would go well with the lion-skin rug he was having imported, and his favorite part were the walls he'd painted red. The decor hanging from them was all gold, real gold, and so was the chandelier hanging from the tall ceiling. He'd acquired his father's taste of preferring the finer things in life, and now he simply couldn't live without them. The other traits he got from his father was his love for women and money, but unfortunately that was where the similarities stopped.

Laron had wanted Leon to walk the path that he himself laid out for his son. He didn't care that it wasn't what Leon wanted. When Leon graduated high school, he sent him to college for agriculture so he could one day take his place on the family farm. Laron told him it was the business that would keep their family rich forever. At the time, Leon didn't know what he wanted to do, but he knew it wasn't that. But still, he obliged his father, because Laron was right. There was a lot of money in farming, and it was something they already owned. That and their family house. Leaving Tina was hard to do. Especially knowing how Laron treated her. When he got older, he got bigger and stronger, while his father got older and slower. He'd stopped several beatings Laron had tried to bestow on Tina. She was the only woman he had ever loved, and with him gone, there would be nobody there to protect her. But even she had told him that he should leave.

"Go get your degree, baby. Use everything, good and bad, that Laron has shown you, and when you come back, you'll be a greater man than he could ever be."

Those were the words she'd said to him, and he always wondered if she knew he would take them literally. He attended school in Texas, where the family farm was, so he could work hands-on while in school. He never understood why he was expected to work on the farm when his father moved to Florida the first chance he could. Still, it was all good until he realized that he was only working for experience and no money was involved. Laron only sent him a certain amount to eat every month, and since Leon wasn't in school on scholarship, there was no yearly school check. That was how he ended up pimping his first girl out. He needed the money, and she was so in love with him she would do anything. Her name was Nicole Bradford, but everyone called her CoCo for short. She was the hottest thing on campus, and everybody wanted a piece of her, but Leon was the one who got her.

One night the two of them got stranded on a desolate road in her car. It was a terrible rainstorm, and the roads had started to flood. After hours of no cars, a trucker finally stopped. He took one look at CoCo and said that the only way he would give them a lift back into town was if she gave him a blowjob. At first Leon contested it, not wanting anyone to touch his woman. But then the trucker offered $100.

"It's okay, baby, I'll do it," CoCo said. "There's no telling if any other cars will pass by, and with the roads flooding, we can't stay here. We don't even have cell service."

"CoCo . . ." Leon said and glared at the trucker, who was watching them from his truck.

"Baby, we need the money," she told him. "We already spent the two hundred dollars your dad sent, and I haven't been making any tips at the restaurant. You have a midterm tomorrow. I'm not gonna let you miss it if there is something I can do about it. I'd do anything for you, anything."

"Okay," Leon finally sighed. He didn't like it, but at the moment, he didn't see any other choice. Laron would stop sending money altogether if he failed a course. *"Okay. But make sure he puts on protection."*

"Okay," CoCo said and made to get out of the car but paused. She looked back at him with concern written in her eyes. *"Leon, promise me this won't change things between us. You're all I have in this world since the house fire."*

"It won't," Leon told her. "I'll be here waiting for you."

Leon had of course been lying, but that was only the first of many promises he would break. After that first time, Leon realized his father had been right. Make a woman feel like she couldn't live without you, and not only would she never leave you, but she would do anything to keep you. CoCo's entire family had died in a house fire, and nobody in the world but Leon knew it was her fault. She'd been smoking a cigarette in the garage while her parents were asleep, and instead of putting it out with her shoe, she flicked it in an old supply box, thinking it would go out on its own. It didn't, and her whole family suffered for what she'd done. Leon was the only person she felt she had, and she proved she would do whatever for him.

He never did feel the same way about her after the first time, and that made it easier to let her sell her body for him the second time. And the third time. Soon she'd done it so much that he'd lost count, but the money was good. She was so blinded by her love for him she couldn't see that he didn't love her. CoCo was constantly proving her loyalty to him, and for that, he took care of her.

When he graduated after four years of being away, he took her back home to Florida with him. He knew his dad wanted him to stay and help run the farm, but he wasn't ready to do that just yet. He'd found a new hustle, and he wanted to live off that for a while. But what he didn't know was that the home he was coming back to wasn't a home anymore at all. It was a war zone. Leon balled one of his hands in a fist thinking about that first day back. It was the second day that changed his life.

"Pops, I'm home. I have somebody I want you to meet!" Leon called in the house when he came through the front door.

"Damn, this door is heavy!" CoCo commented, holding it open with her back so she could pull her luggage through.

"My pops did that so he could always hear if someone was coming or going. There ain't no way that door can close quietly," Leon told her and then went back to yelling for his father. "Pops! I'm home!"

He went up the circular staircase and toward the master bedroom, thinking that maybe Laron and Tina were still sleeping, although it was late afternoon. CoCo followed closely behind him like a lost puppy. Leon knew something was awry the second he got to the second level of the house. His eyes instantly went to the holes in the hallway walls that led to their bedroom. There was also a smudge of blood.

"What the . . ." CoCo said, wide-eyed, looking at the damage.

"Stay here," he instructed her and ran toward the cracked door.

It felt like his heart was about to jump out of his chest. He just knew when he opened the bedroom door, he was going to find Tina dead because Laron had finally snapped. But when he burst through the doors, it was the exact opposite. Laron was lying on the ground in front of their California-king bed, writhing in pain, while Tina stood over him with a knife. It looked like a fight had ensued in the bedroom as well, being that there was stuff knocked over everywhere. Laron had suffered a stab wound to the side, and Tina was breathing heavily over him. She wasn't without injury herself. Her left eye was badly swollen, and both her nose and mouth were bleeding. It pained Leon to see her pretty face in such a state.

"Tina," he said.

She looked in a daze in his direction. She blinked her eyes a few times and snapped out of her trance. A look of surprise came over her face when she saw Leon standing there.

"Leon? What are you doing here, babe?"

"I told y'all I was coming home today. What happened, Tina?" Leon asked, pointing at the knife in her hand.

She looked down at the knife and then at Laron. A gasp escaped through her lips, and she dropped the knife. Tina put her hands to her mouth, and she shook her head as if she couldn't believe what she had done.

"Oh, no. No, no, no, no, no."

"What happened, Tina? Tell me. I won't be mad at you."

"Son," Laron said weakly from the bed. *"Call the police. Call them. She just tried to kill me."*

Leon ignored his father. He took a step toward Tina and put his hands on her shoulders. When she looked up at him, she had tears streaming down her face.

"I didn't mean to. He . . ."

"What did he do?" Leon asked and glared briefly down at where his father lay bleeding.

"He was drinking again, and he got angry with me because I was getting your room ready instead of folding his laundry. He said I always cared more about you than him, and the next thing I knew, he was beating me all down the hallway."

"Is that why there's blood on the walls? That's your blood?"

"Yes. He slid my face on the wall after he bashed my head into it."

"How did this happen?" Leon asked and pointed at Laron.

"I . . ." Tina looked down at Laron, and her eyes were frozen on the blood spilling onto the wooden floor. *"Oh, my God. I'm going to jail."*

"You're not going to jail. Just talk to me."

"I hid a knife in here after our last big fight. And when we got in here, I grabbed it. I grabbed it and stabbed him before he could hurt me some more. Oh God, Leon. What am I gonna do? I can't go to jail!"

"You're not. I won't let them take you," Leon assured her gently, grabbing both sides of her face. *"You hear me? I won't let them take you."*

"What are you gonna do?"

"You let me worry about that. There is somebody in the hallway. Go with her. Tell her I said to call 911 and report a domestic dispute."

"If you do that, they're gonna take me. He'll lie like he always does, and they'll believe him like they always do!"

"He can't talk if he's unconscious," Leon said, raising his brows at her. "Now go."

She nodded her head and left the room. Leon turned back to where his father lay struggling to catch his breath. Anyone else might not have seen the difference between him and Laron. They both made a woman do what they told them, and if they got out of line, they used physical force. But the difference was that Leon would never do that to the woman he loved, only his property. And that was what CoCo was. Tina was the only mother Leon had ever known. The love he had for her went beyond skin and blood, and that would be the last time Laron would be able to hurt her.

"Son, help me. I'm dying," Laron pleaded with his son.

The last twenty-one years of Leon's life passed in front of his eyes. The beatings, the control Laron had over his life, and the fact that he never made Leon feel good enough. Laron was his father, but he had never really been his dad. That realization made what Leon was about to do all the simpler.

"No," Leon said right before he hit Laron hard enough in his head to knock him out until the police came.

When they did come, Tina told them that she had only pulled out the knife to scare Laron from hitting her anymore. And Leon told them that he heard the commotion when he walked in and ran to their room. Once he got there, Leon said he saw Laron rush toward Tina in a fit of anger, and he ran right into the knife. When Laron felt that he'd been stabbed, he fell to the ground, hitting his head on the bed, and passed out. The police said that they couldn't take Tina to jail without getting Laron's input on what happened, so she could stay in the home for now. Leon was fine with that because he knew Tina would be just fine. He didn't have any plans of letting his father ever wake up or talk to anybody again.

When Leon came back to reality, he had a twisted smile on his face. His father's life was the first one he ever took, and it changed him forever. He was meaner, colder . . . well, to everyone but Tina. She was proud of what he had become and constantly wrote him to tell him that. She was somewhere living happily in California. She moved shortly after Laron died. Leon told her she was more than welcome to stay, but she declined. She said the house had too many bad memories for her. Although he was sad to see her leave after being in his life for so long, he wanted her to live the rest of her life the way she wanted. He sent her money every month just so she wouldn't have to work. It was strange, really, that he would let go of the only person he loved, but he'd hold tightly on to the ones he didn't care about. It was something not even he understood. He just knew they were his, now and forever.

He sat in the office and visualized the opening night of the Fantasy Factory for a little while longer before deciding to go home. The girls had been working hard. Even Anissa had started to fall in line. He'd forbidden her to work until the opening of the gentlemen's club, so she made herself useful around the house. He walked into a sparkling clean home and already-made dinner every day. Leon felt that it was finally time to break her in as he had done with all his girls. They, on the other hand, had thrown themselves at him. But when he slept with them, there was no emotion there. No feeling. Just human masturbation devices. But with Anissa? He didn't want her to feel as if she was doing a job by screwing him.

He wanted her to want it. To feel it. To *love* it and in turn love him. He wanted her devotion, which was why he hadn't laid a finger on her . . . yet.

When he got to the house, he walked into what he had expected. It was squeaky clean, and he could barely smell the clean linen scent over the delicious aroma coming from the kitchen. As soon as the door closed behind him, he heard feet scurrying toward the stairs. Not too long after that, he saw Angel, Harmony, and CoCo coming down them. They were dressed casually since he had been giving them some time off before the gentlemen's club opened. He had to make their usual tricks miss them so that they would be eager to see them at the Fantasy Factory. CoCo had the biggest smile of all of them when she spotted him.

"Daddy, I missed you," she cooed. "After we eat, don't forget it's my night with you."

"Actually, I was thinking I would spend the night with him," Anissa's voice sounded.

Leon turned his head just in time to see her walking out of the kitchen. She was wearing only an apron, a thong, and a pair of high heels that showed off her freshly manicured toes. Her face and hair had been dolled up as if she had gotten pretty just for him. He thought his eyes were deceiving him, but when he blinked, she was still there.

"And I thought that maybe the other girls could take their plates to their rooms for tonight," she said, looking hopefully at Leon. "If that's okay with you."

"Anything for you, queen," Leon said. "CoCo, Harmony, and Angel, go make your plates, and stay in your rooms for the rest of the night."

"But, daddy, it's *my* night," CoCo whined but was silenced instantly when Leon shot her a deathly stare.

As she headed toward the kitchen, she had a pained expression on her face that turned into a look of contempt when she passed Anissa. Anissa, unchallenged, retuned the look with a smile of her own. Her confidence was sexy.

While CoCo, Angel, and Harmony made their plates, Anissa led Leon to his usual seat at the head of the table. When he sat down, she sensually ran her hand across his chest while she went to make his plate. He watched her ass jiggle as she walked away and felt the same feeling in his chest that he'd felt the first time he saw her in the club. Like he *had* to have her.

"That's enough. Get out," he instructed the three who weren't supposed to be there. They cleared out instantly with their plates in tow, and when they were gone, Leon rubbed his hands together. "So, what did you whip us up for dinner tonight, queen?"

"I made them some chicken and waffles, but for *you*"—Anissa came back to the table and set a hot plate down in front of him—"I made roast and potatoes with a side of my special green beans. I had that roast slow-cooking all day now, so you better eat it all."

"If it's as good as you look right now, I will," Leon said to her, giving her his bedroom eyes.

"If you eat it all, I might let you eat something else tonight," she said, turning around and bending over.

"Goddamn," Leon heard himself say as he watched her huge ass cheeks open and close over the little piece of fabric between them. "I'ma eat all of this then."

"Good." Anissa beamed at him and went to make herself a plate of chicken and waffles. When she returned, she sat in the seat closest to him on the right. "How was your day?"

"It was cool," Leon said, taking a big bite of his roast and mashed potatoes. "Goddamn, this is good. You might give CoCo a run for her money in the kitchen. If I had known you could throw down like this, you woulda been cooking for me with that ass out."

"Thank you, baby. Better late than never, right?" Anissa said and sexily bit her lip at him.

"What I'm tryin'a figure out, though, is what caused the complete three-sixty? You've been different lately from when you first got here."

"I just figured that if this is my life now, maybe I should just make the best of it," Anissa said softly and batted her eyelashes at him. "I mean, you're good to me and buy me whatever I want. Isn't that what most girls want in a man?"

"So, it was my gifts that won you over?"

"And the fact that I've always thought you were so sexy. I guess the thought of sharing you with three other women used to make me jealous, so I acted stupid. Now I see it's not so bad, and I don't want to make you mad. You work so hard to take care of us."

The words coming out of Anissa's mouth were like heaven to his ears. But Leon was born at night, but not last night. He stared curiously at Anissa, trying to figure out her game plan. She wanted something, but he didn't know what.

"Just come out and say it," he told her, taking another bite of food.

"Say what?" she asked innocently.

"What it is you want. The attire, the food. Shit, the way you're talking to me is a dead giveaway, shawty," he said, and she sighed.

"Okay, okay. I'm caught," she said, rolling her eyes. "I *did* want to ask you for something."

"That is?"

"I wanted to go see my cousin in the hospital," Anissa said, and when Leon paused in his chewing, she sped through the rest of her statement. "It's just, I haven't seen her the whole time I've been here, and the doctors are saying she is showing signs of finally waking up. I just want to be there when she does. And . . ."

"And what?"

"The detective working her case called me the other night."

"Called you? Damn, I forgot I never took your phone," Leon commented more to himself than to her. "Continue."

"He said that when she wakes up, they can finally question her, because by the way she was shot, they know she was forward facing. Which means she probably saw who her shooter was!" she said happily.

Leon looked into her smiling face with a stricken expression of his own. He'd been so busy getting everything ready for his club that Brynn had been pushed to the back of his mind. That and the fact that she had been in a coma for so long. He should have finished the job a long time ago. No matter, he would handle it. But in the meantime, he wanted to keep the smile on Anissa's face. He quickly fixed his expression and forced a smile to his lips.

"Anything for you, queen. We can go on Friday."

"Why not tomorrow?" Anissa asked, and Leon's eyes flashed. She saw the look and quickly backed off. "Friday it is."

"Good," Leon said and went back to eating his food. It was so good that by the time he was finished, his plate looked like it had been licked clean. He pushed the plate away and watched Anissa pick at her food for a moment. "You know what I'm thinking?"

"What?" she asked.

"That the entire time you've been in this house, it's been me doing things for you. Now it's time for you to do something for me."

"Something like what?" Anissa asked, even though they both knew what he was talking about.

"You think me seeing you looking like that wasn't gon' make my dick hard?" he asked, massaging his crotch. "He needs some attention right now."

"Right now?" Anissa asked, watching Leon push his chair away from the table and unzip his slacks.

"Right now," he confirmed and whipped out his nine-inch, thick piece of meat.

He pushed his pants and boxers to his ankles and motioned for Anissa to get on her knees. She was a little hesitant, but she did it. The sight of her on her knees in front of him made him feel powerful, like he had broken the hardest bitch in the game. She stared his one-eyed monster down before finally wrapping her full, glossy lips around it.

"Oooh, shit," he moaned, feeling the warmth of her mouth down his shaft.

It went all the way to the back of her mouth, and she didn't gag. In fact, he felt her throat trying to swallow the tip of his dick, all while massaging her tongue on him. It felt so good that he wanted to close his eyes, but he couldn't because he wanted to watch as well. Anissa commenced giving him the best head he'd ever received. The mix of the sound of her throating him with the feeling was so good to him that he had to clutch the sides of his chair. Leon moaned and tried to get control over himself, but he couldn't. He was completely at her mercy. Not once did he feel her teeth, and not once did it hurt when she was playing with his balls. She was a pro, and he had to know what her pussy felt like before he exploded.

"Sit on it," he demanded and pointed at his soaked manhood.

"Okay, daddy," she said, and he moaned again.

"That sounds so good coming from your mouth," he told her as she straddled him and moved her thong to the side. He moved her long hair out of her face to cup her cheek softly and look into her eyes. Once he felt his tip at her hole, he forced his way in a tiny bit, and she hissed. "I'm not gon' treat you like them other bitches, okay? You're special to me."

"Okay," she whispered as he battled against her tightness.

"I've been wanting this for so long, shit. I'm gon' take my time with it," he told her breathily.

His meat was throbbing to be completely inside of her, but still he inserted himself slowly, watching all the little changes in her face. Pain. Bliss. Pleasure. When he was completely inside, he gripped her hips and ground her down so she could feel how deep he was.

"Ohh! Leon!"

"That's not my name," he reminded her.

"I'm sorry, daddy."

"It's okay. I'm about to make you remember," he said and kissed her perfect chin. "Pretty soon, daddy's name is gon' be written all over this tight pussy."

He untied the apron she was wearing and pulled it over her head so that he could see her pretty nipples. She began to ride him slowly, making her breasts jiggle and in turn making him harder against her walls. His mouth found its way to her areolas, where he licked and sucked while her pussy ate him alive. Her moans were music to his ears, and he felt her growing wetter and wetter.

When he was done munching on her breasts, Leon forced Anissa to lean her chest into him and rest her head on his shoulder. He gripped her cheeks with both hands, opening them wide before he began to thrust violently up into her. Her hands held tightly on to the back of his chair as she tried to take the hammering he was giving to her. But it was too much to bear. She screamed and quivered as she let go of her first orgasm. He felt her walls clench and unclench around him, and it turned him on even more. He knocked everything on the table to the floor in a loud crash and plopped Anissa down without ever sliding out of.

Anissa was thick, and the way she wiggled when their bodies met made him bite his lips. For men, sex was felt, but it was more visual than anything. She was as beautiful as she was sexy, and if he could stay inside of her forever, he would. Leon had never had shaky knees while fucking a woman before, but he had to hold on to her legs for support or he would have fallen over.

"Anissa, you gon' make me fall in love with this pussy," he moaned in a grimace.

Their eyes were locked on each other's, and he could tell she felt as good as he did. She had one hand going back and forth pinching her nipples while the other one rubbed her glistening clit. Suddenly, he pulled out of her and forced her thighs to open more with his hands. He licked his lips and buried his face between her legs. He rubbed his face all in her juices before he began to lick and suck away. Her body quivered, and he ignored her when she asked for clemency. She was his, and he didn't plan on stopping until he was good and ready. While he ate her deliciousness, he stroked himself.

"I don't know if I can let anybody in this ever," he said between licks. "But this shit is fire. It's gon' make us so much money."

"Daddy," she moaned, "I'm about to cum."

"I'll nut with you, baby."

Leon stopped licking and slid back inside of her. She sat up and scooted to the edge of the table so she could hungrily match him stroke for stroke. She was so warm and gushy, Leon couldn't stand it. When he felt his eruption coming, he wrapped a hand around her neck and gripped it. Not too hard, but hard enough to where she couldn't get away from him.

"Oh, oh, shit! It's heeeere!" she screamed and splashed her juices all over his torso.

Leon felt himself release at the same time and pulled out, squirting his semen all over her chunky cat. His dick jumped until it had been completely drained, and when he was done, he fell back into his chair. That orgasm took more out of him than his normal climaxes, and he was suddenly very tired. He tried to catch his breath, but it felt like he couldn't. He tried to focus on Anissa as she got up from the table, but he swore he saw two of her. Blinking didn't help.

"Come on, daddy," she said in a distorted voice. "Let's go have some more fun in your room. I know you aren't one and done, are you?"

"Hell nah," Leon said and let her help him to his feet. "I just need to lie down for a minute."

"All right, daddy."

He half walked and half stumbled with her to the stairs. If what she had between her legs made him feel like that after one round, he knew he had been right. He had landed on a gold mine.

Chapter 15

When Leon woke up the next morning, he felt amazing. A little dizzy, but other than that, amazing. He looked over and saw that Anissa was still in his bed sound asleep. She had given him the best sex he'd had in a while, and from the way they had rocked out all night, he knew why she was so tired. He checked the digital clock and saw that it read just before eleven in the morning. Leon wanted to wake her up and get some more sex, because later she might not be in the mood. After he handled his unfinished business, she might not be in the mood for a lot. Knowing that time was of the essence, Leon decided to leave her sleeping and got out of bed, careful not to wake her.

He stepped over the spot where his father had been all those years ago, bleeding on the ground, to get to the closet. He picked out a gray tailored suit to wear and opted against putting in his gold teeth that day. After showering, getting dressed, and brushing his hair, he left. On his way to his destination, he stopped and grabbed some flowers. He figured they would be a nice parting gift for Brynn.

By the time he got to the hospital, it was just after noon, and it was busy. The nurse told him Brynn's room number and allowed him to go back without having him sign in. Leon hummed to himself as he walked with one hand in his pants pocket and the other one swinging the flowers. When he got to her room, he checked his surroundings before smiling to himself and entering. Brynn was hooked up to a machine that monitored her heart rate and was lying motionless with her eyes closed.

"Long time no see," Leon said to her unconscious body. "You should really be in a grave by now. I won't let you take her from me."

He set the flowers down at the foot of her bed and made his way to the tray by her IV. The doctor must have just given her some morphine because there was a syringe with a needle on it. Maybe it wasn't even morphine, but whatever it was, Leon was sure that too much of it would kill her.

"I'm sure your body has been through so much pain at this point," he said to her like she could hear him. "Let me take you out of your misery."

He popped the top on the IV and checked the window on the door to make sure no one was passing by at that moment. He then tried to administer the medicine through the IV. However, he didn't get the chance to. The door to the hospital room swung open, and suddenly he was surrounded by police officers who had their guns pointed his way.

"Put the needle down and put your hands up where I can see them!"

Leon looked at the man who had just shouted at him and guessed he was a detective and not a regular cop. He was wearing a suit and giving him a glare like he was the scum of the universe. Confused, Leon dropped the syringe and did what he was told. How could they have known he would be there to kill Brynn? He hadn't told anyone. It wasn't until Anissa entered the room wearing a big smile that he understood. If it hadn't been for the eight guns pointed at him, he would have strangled her the same way he'd done to Bubbles. He wanted to wipe the smug look off her face for good. How could she have done that to him?

"Leon, let me formally introduce you to Detective Evans," Anissa said, motioning to the man in the brown suit. "We set this whole thing up. I called him as soon as you left this morning, and we came here together."

"You dirty bitch," Leon snarled.

"You thought I was gonna just let you get away with trying to kill my cousin?" she asked. "And by the way, the room was wired. They heard everything."

"Maybe so, but that's not enough to hold up in court. Plus, Brynn is still in a coma. They can't lock me up without her statement," Leon told her as an officer roughly put his hands behind his back and cuffed him.

"You're right," Detective Evans stated and then pointed toward Brynn. "I guess it's a good thing she came out of her coma two days ago."

Leon's eyes widened as he whirled his head to look at Brynn. Sure enough, she was alert and staring at him with vengeful eyes. Leon was so taken aback that he was at a loss for words.

"I hope they rape you every single day, you son of a bitch," Brynn said in a hoarse voice.

At that moment, Anissa walked up to Leon and spoke to him in a voice that only he could hear. "So about last night, it was great, huh?" she asked.

"I should have known you were up to something."

"The funny thing is, this isn't all I did." Anissa beamed. "The food was amazing last night, wasn't it? Did you wake up a little dizzy this morning?"

Leon thought back to how unlike himself he'd felt the night before. It was the same that morning. He'd thought it was just from having great sex, but the look on Anissa's face told him that something else might have been at play.

"You drugged me." He was astonished.

"Yup, and we did have sex again, I can't even lie. You have some good dick. What a waste to be attached to such a piece of shit," she said, shaking her head. "But before then we did something else. Or should I say, *you* did something else. You signed over ownership of the Fantasy Factory to me, *and* the deed to the building. *And* you transferred all the money you currently have in your bank account to me. Damn, it's crazy what good pussy does to a nigga."

She stepped back when he viciously lurched toward her. It took two officers to hold him back from getting to her. A look of fear crossed over her face, but it was gone faster than it came. She went over to Brynn and let the officers take him away.

"This isn't over," he said over his shoulder.

"But I do believe it is," Detective Evans said and began reading him his Miranda rights.

Chapter 16

One Year Later

Click clack, click clack.

The sounds of Anissa's Louboutins stabbing the lino-
leum floors were the only sounds echoing on the walls as
she walked down the long, desolate hallway. She passed
many soundproof doors on the way to one, and when she
got there, she opened the door without knocking. The
scene she saw when the door swung open upset her so
much that it almost showed on her face. A young naked
woman was cowering in the corner of a nicely decked-out
small lounge room, while a tall white man stood over
her. He was still dressed, but his suit jacket was off, and
the back of his neck had sweat beads. When Anissa had
opened the door, she'd witnessed him striking the girl.
Her girl. When the man raised his hand to land another
blow, Anissa cleared her throat. He turned around,
allowing her to witness the look of pure rage on his face.
Her eyes flickered around the room, and she saw a silver
tray next to the red couch that cocaine was served on.
Anissa didn't know how much he'd partaken in, but it
had to have been a lot, because minus a little dusting of
the drug, the tray was empty. She averted her eyes back
to him, and she waved her fingers at him.

"Mr. Petroli, you know the rules. Minus a few kinky
taps, being violent toward any of my Fantasy girls is not

permitted," she told him with a solid expression on her face.

Terrance Petroli was a new member to the Fantasy Factory. He was a well-known restaurant chain owner in Florida and someone who put his money where his mouth was. He'd become a white card member, and Anissa quickly took notice of his drug addiction. He didn't have a favorite girl when he came, which wasn't uncommon, and the cocaine made him tip generously. It was a habit that had made him an asset to the Fantasy girls, and there was always a rush for one of them to get to him first. However, Buttercup didn't know what was going to be in store for her when she disappeared into one of the fantasy rooms with him that evening.

"I wasn't hurtin' her," Terrance lied.

Anissa looked back at Buttercup, who had a look of fear in her eyes. She also saw a bruise forming on her pretty face. Anissa breathed in deeply and let out a long sigh.

"You were doing something to her that made her hit the panic button," Anissa told him and motioned to the button above where Buttercup kneeled. "Buttercup, go get cleaned up. Close the door behind you."

"Yes, my lady." Butter cup nodded, jumping gladly to her feet.

"But I'm not through with her yet!" Terrance tried to grab for Buttercup.

"Yes, you are." Anissa sent him an icy look that made him stop mid-reach.

He scoffed and let his arm fall. "Well, are *you* gonna suck my dick, sweetheart?" he asked once the two of them were alone.

His comment tickled her almost as much as the smug expression on his face. So many men were just like him. They thought they could do whatever and treat women however they wanted just because they were men. They thought that just by being a man, they had power. But that wasn't factual. True power came from within.

"Unfortunately, I am not gonna suck your dick, Mr. Petroli. I own this place. I don't work here. You, however, could have had a fantastic time had you not felt the need to lay hands on Buttercup. Your membership is hereby revoked. Please leave."

"What? Bitch, you're crazy. I just spent twenty thousand dollars on my membership!"

"And you won't be getting a penny back. You've probably snorted that much in cocaine since the beginning of the month." Anissa's voice was unapologetic. "I won't ask you again to leave."

"Whore, you're running an illegal sex business in the middle of town. I'll go to the police and get this place shut down! Then I'll have you thrown in jail."

Anissa stared into his serious face as he pointed an angry finger into hers. Everything about his body language was hilarious to her, so she laughed. She laughed so hard that his pale face turned red.

"You? Shut me down?" she asked. "See, there is a reason we confiscate your phone and any recording devices you might have for the time you're here until the time you're out the doors. Also, don't you think I have my i's dotted and my t's crossed when it comes to the police? I'll be alerted days before anyone shows up at my place of business. And the only proof you'll ever have is a system drowned in cocaine that you could have gotten from anywhere."

Terrance was baffled. His mouth opened and shut repeatedly before he finally gave up. He snatched his suit jacket from the couch before angrily heading for the door.

"Oh, and Mr. Petroli?" she asked as he passed her.

"Wha—"

Anissa's hard backhand caught him hard in the face. The rings on her fingers sliced through his skin, and he fell to the ground. He tried to get up and rush her, but Anissa brandished a small firearm from the holster on her waist.

"That was for hurting my girls," she said and cocked the gun. "And this will be for trying to hurt me. If I ever see your face around here again, you're a dead man."

Seeing the gun pointed at his face was enough motivation for him to want to get far away from her. He got to his feet and beelined to the exit. Anissa put the gun back on her hip and fixed the jacket of her own form-fitting black pants suit so that the weapon was hidden again. Next, she pulled out her cell phone and made a call to Trent, the head of her security. He was a dude from the streets and did whatever Anissa said to do.

"What's up, my lady?" his gruff voice said when he answered.

"Terrance Petroli is coming down. Be sure that his membership to the Fantasy Factory is revoked. Also, please give him a *mean* reminder of why we don't hit girls."

"You got it."

She disconnected the call and exited the room and went back to her office. The royal decor always made her feel high and mighty when she walked through. The only thing she changed were the red walls. They were now arctic white. She sat down behind her club-footed desk in her throne chair. She loved how the room complemented the title she'd given herself. She was royalty, and despite her past, she had always thought of herself as such, so she made everyone refer to her as "my lady," as they did every great queen.

She scooted her chair to her desk in front of her computer monitors. On them there were many little boxes of surveillance videos from all her Fantasy rooms, including the front room for silver members. Although she did have cameras in all the rooms, there was no way that she alone could monitor what was happening at every second, which was why she'd installed panic buttons in all the rooms for the girls. Anissa had been in the middle of going through that month's income statements when Buttercup called, and that was what she went back to doing.

Anissa sifted through the paperwork in front of her and felt overwhelmingly pleased about the success of the Fantasy Factory in its first year of being open. Although the idea of it all had been Leon's, Anissa had made it what it was. His business plan had so many holes in it, holes that a man could never see. Like installing the panic button for starters. And making sure that the chief of police was one of her most prominent members. Leon would have never been able to pull that off because he was so lost in his own fantasy world of thinking he was untouchable. Anissa had also installed microphones in every room and had learned the secrets of all the important businessmen who indulged in the Fantasy Factory. It was amazing what secrets pussy could coax out of a man without even trying to.

Although only a year had gone by, life had changed drastically for Anissa, and she wasn't the same girl she used to be. In that time frame, she'd gone from a young escort to a millionaire. Before, she had only been looking at the smaller picture: make enough money to maintain her high-fashion addiction. But now she was focused on the bigger picture: expansion. Anissa now had over twenty girls working for her, and they were able to live high-end lives because of her. She wanted to open a Fantasy Factory in Atlanta, where she was from, and maybe even move back home. Maybe have Harmony run the one in Florida, since Brynn had gone back to running her own business. Brynn probably wouldn't have agreed to it anyway. She had left that life behind her. When Anissa extended a partnership to her, Brynn respectfully declined. She said that when Leon almost killed her, it put a lot into perspective for her about things. It made her appreciate life enough to only do the things she enjoyed doing. She wanted to leave everything about selling sex in the past. So, Anissa left it alone. As long as they were still able to meet up every Sunday for brunch despite any busy schedule, that was okay with her.

So that left Harmony. She'd helped Anissa put Leon in jail, and for that she gained Anissa's trust. Anissa could even say that she had become something like a close friend to her in the past year. So close that Harmony was no longer a working girl. She was more like a partner with her own office and all. She kept the girls in line and provided council for them whenever they needed someone to talk to. She, however, was the only one who adapted without problem to her new life.

After surviving Leon, Anissa wanted Harmony, Angel, and even CoCo to come work for her. She promised things would be different and that they would make a lot of money. Harmony was instantly on board, but Angel didn't have that same kind of faith in Anissa. She didn't think she could pull it off without Leon, and she wanted to live her own life. Anissa hadn't seen or heard from her since.

CoCo, on the other hand, had a hard time detaching from Leon. But when the reality hit that he was facing twenty years in prison, she finally agreed to come work for Anissa. She wasn't happy when Anissa gave Harmony a position higher than hers, but Anissa told her she'd have to prove her loyalty in order to move up in the ranks. She banned her from ever going to visit Leon and told her that if she did, she would be kicked out of the gentlemen's club for good. Anissa hoped that since a year had passed, maybe he was finally out of her system completely.

She focused her attention to one of the boxes on one of her computer monitors and watched one of CoCo's regulars walk into a Fantasy room. He had a tray of cocaine in his hands, and when he sat down to wait for her, he loosened his tie and snorted a line instantly. He wasn't just addicted to the drugs, he was addicted to CoCo, just like a few other members. Anissa didn't know what kind of spell she put on her clients, but it must have been something, because they refused to ever spend time with another girl. Anissa smirked to herself and went back to going over her statements.

For the past year, CoCo's heart played a vicious game of tug of war with her brain. She knew that she was better off without Leon. She knew that he had been manipulating her for years. She knew all of that, but still her heart longed for him at times. In the beginning of him being gone, CoCo had terrible "daddy" withdrawal. It was like a fiend trying to let go of their favorite drug. There were days she couldn't eat and or drink anything. There were nights she woke up in cold sweats expecting to see him standing at the foot of her bed ready to punish her for betraying him. She hadn't been without him since before her college days, and at first, she didn't know how to act without him.

CoCo hated Anissa at first. She was sitting on a throne that Leon had designed for himself and reaping all the benefits of his hard work. How could she do that to someone who just wanted to take care of all of them? When Anissa banned her from seeing Leon and told her she would be cut off if she did, CoCo felt like a helpless child. But the more time she spent away from Leon, the more she realized that not being able to see him was the only thing she wasn't allowed to do. Anissa had given her complete control back over her life. She'd even gotten her a car. Working for the Fantasy Factory was always a choice for her, not something she was being forced to do. It felt good. She didn't remember the last time she was able to leave without checking in. Anissa told all her girls that if she offered enough perks, she knew they would always come back.

"That's what a boss who appreciates their employees does. As long as you work here, I will always show you girls love."

That was something Anissa always said. She had become the ultimate pimp and had done something no other had. She ran a complete facility off of love and kindness. She didn't let anyone harm her girls or cheat them out of their money. She even gave them each rotating weeks off so that they could travel and experience life.

"I don't expect you girls to work for me forever. I want you to experience love and true happiness. And if with the money you make here you end up finding that, then that means I did my job as your lady."

That was something Anissa often said as well. Without even noticing, the malice CoCo had in the beginning toward Anissa slowly faded away until it was almost nonexistent. She still had bouts of missing Leon, but if she had the choice between freedom and bondage, the decision would be easy. Deep down she knew Anissa's version of the Fantasy Factory was better than what Leon's would have been. He would have overworked them and not given them a dime, even though he said he would have.

CoCo found herself constantly calling to check in until Anissa told her to stop doing so. Once was okay, but every hour was a little much. She didn't realize how true that statement was until she really thought about it. However, she'd been so used to that being one of Leon's rules that it proved to be a hard habit to break. She also thought about the fact that she was Leon's oldest girl, but whenever he could, he put whatever new girl he obtained before her. Angel, Harmony, and then Anissa. And look at where that had gotten him. Locked away. Maybe for good. Hopefully for good.

"This is your new life," she said out loud to herself as she stared at her reflection in the mirror. "Get used to it."

She urged herself to hurry up in the dressing room, because she'd been requested in one of the private rooms in the Fantasy Factory. She was wearing a cute little latex number that barely covered anything on her shapely body. She tied the matching leather mask over her eyes and scooped her hair into a messy bun. Once she was done, she walked down a long hall until she found the door that had her name on it. When she walked in, there was a portly white man inside patiently waiting for her. His name was Alan, and in the weeks they'd been open, he'd quickly become one of her regulars. She didn't mind it because he tipped well and always came back for more. He wasn't an ugly man, but he wasn't a looker either. He was a politician who was used to getting anything he wanted just because he had money and, well, he'd come to the right place for that.

He sat on the plush couch and gulped down air when he saw CoCo in her getup. Next to him on a glass table was a silver tray with a line of cocaine on it. She could tell by the hunger in his eyes that he'd already done one line—that and the power residue around his nostril.

"Back for another round already," she said with a smile. "I thought I just saw you yesterday, Alan."

"I don't think I can get enough of you," he admitted to her. "I'm addicted to you, CoCo. You give me a high higher than this fucking cocaine."

"You aren't addicted to me. You're addicted to this chocolate pussy," CoCo told him.

"I do love it. Can I have it? My wife just doesn't give it to me like you."

"What doesn't she do for you, Alan?"

"She just lies there," he said, demonstrating with his hands. "Like a fucking log. And her body is nowhere near as fun as yours."

"You must know that I love flattery. And because of that, yes, you can have it."

"I can?" he asked, licking his lips with his short tongue.

"That's what you're here for, right? So, I can give it to you?" CoCo turned around and put her bottom in his face. "You love it when I do that, don't you, naughty boy?"

"Oh, yeah. I love having this big black ass in my face. Have you been a naughty girl?"

"I think so." She looked back at him and feigned a pout.

He smacked one of her cheeks harder than she would have liked him to. But she didn't react. She was there for him to use, so she just moaned like she liked it. He smacked the other cheek the next time and then quickly moved her thick leather thong to the side to shove his tongue in her anus. That was one thing she liked about him. He got straight to the point. Some of the others liked to sit and talk about their family life and other things CoCo didn't give a damn about. She was there to fuck them and suck them dry, not to be their counselor. But Anissa told them all that building personal relationships with them was how to keep them coming back. Make them feel like they had a friend. Alan didn't care about having a friend. He just wanted to get his little six-inch dick wet. But CoCo had to admit he knew how to work his tongue.

A moan escaped her mouth as he ate her ass like a hot fudge sundae. She opened both cheeks and let them crash on both sides of his face. She did that a few times, wondering if he would cum before they even had sex like he'd done the day before. When she heard him fumbling with his belt buckle, she guessed not. She would have to pretend like he had the biggest dick in the universe, even though she knew that he knew it wasn't true.

"You want to give me some of that monster dick?" she asked and looked back at him.

He already had the pink thing out, and it was standing at attention for her. She went over to one of the dressers in the fancy room and pulled a condom from one of the drawers. CoCo ripped it open and slowly rolled it down his shaft.

"You ready to feel the good pussy your wife won't give you, baby?"

"Yes," he said and nodded his head quickly as she slid off her thong.

She straddled him and watched herself through the mirror behind the couch they were on. She had the perfect view of his graying hair and the back of his red neck. She learned that his neck blushed when he was unbelievably horny. CoCo barely felt his small penis slide into her, but she hissed through her teeth like it hurt going in. Alan's eyes instantly rolled to the back of his head when he felt her wetness. CoCo commenced bouncing on him like she was Megan Thee Stallion. He groaned and grunted under her while she pleased him.

"You like this big white cock inside of that black little pussy of yours?" he asked, and she tried not to laugh.

"Mm-hmm," she let out through her pursed lips.

"Let me see these tits. I want them in my mouth while you take my big dick."

He pulled her bra down, releasing her breasts. She felt his mouth kissing and licking all over her nipples, and she tightened her walls around his shaft. She was ready for him to cum. She hadn't taken a lunch break that day, and she was hungry. Her mind was elsewhere when finally, his body turned rigid as he released his semen into the condom.

"Was it good for you, baby?" she asked when she climbed off him.

"Always," he breathed. "You just earned yourself a nice tip."

He dug in his pocket and handed her a big wad of money She counted it and smiled big.

"Thank you, baby. You're so good to me."

"Do you want to do the rest of this coke with me?" he asked with his limp manhood still out.

"No, thank you, but knock yourself out."

"Okay. Can I stay here while I do the line?"

"You're welcome to stay as long as you like. You do have a membership, after all."

She put her thong back on and left him to do his business. All that was on her mind was a toasted roast beef sandwich from the shop fifteen minutes away. She didn't care if Harmony got mad that she was gone. She was starving. Plus, she planned on coming back and working the rest of the day.

CoCo went back into the dressing room and took off the outfit she was wearing. She replaced it with jeans and a hoodie over her perky breasts. Once her shoes were on, she sneaked outside to where her blue 2018 Toyota Camry was parked and got in. As she drove, she figured if she hurried, then Harmony wouldn't know she was gone.

As she drove, she listened to "Pussy Fairy" by Jhene Aiko on repeat and jammed out the whole way. When she danced for her clients, that was her favorite song to dance to. The melody was so smooth and put any customer in the mood to tip well. She got to the sandwich shop in fifteen minutes exactly. When she got out, she didn't bother locking the doors because she was going to be in and right back out. It smelled of delicious breads and meats inside the shop, and the aroma made her stomach growl. She hurried to order the toasted roast beef sandwich she'd been craving before she messed around and ordered the whole menu. In five minutes, she was back outside in her car with her food.

"Oh, my God," she moaned and unwrapped the sandwich. "I'm so hungry!"

She couldn't wait to get back to work to eat. CoCo bit into it and closed her eyes as the flavor erupted against her taste buds. She swallowed that first bite and exhaled, preparing to take another bite. When her eyes opened, they landed on another set of eyes that weren't hers in the rearview mirror. She almost choked and dropped her food when she realized that somebody was sitting in the back seat of her car.

"Long time no see, CoCo. You really shouldn't leave your doors unlocked. Anybody could have gotten in."

It had been years since CoCo had seen the person in her car. In fact, CoCo couldn't even remember the last time she was in Florida.

"Hi, Tina."

Chapter 17

It hadn't been in her plans to come back to the place that had almost broken her, but Tina had no choice. Her loyalty led her back to the very spot that had given her the strength to leave. When Leon called her and told her that they had moved up his trial date, Tina didn't think twice. She went back to Florida. Tina never had children of her own, but she loved Leon like a son so that was the title she gave him. The first place she went to was her old home, the same one that Leon had turned into a whorehouse. She didn't go inside, not only because of the lock on the door, but because she didn't want to come face-to-face with her past. It had taken years for her to lock away the torment Laron had made her endure, and she was afraid that if she went inside, all the power she'd regained over the years would diminish. Tina refused to let the rage win. So, she forced herself not to look at it as her old house, but as Leon's home, a home that he needed to come back to. And the first person she needed to find was CoCo.

Leon told her that there was a possibility that she was working for someone named Anissa at a gentlemen's club, the same club that Leon had been raving to her about for quite some time, the Fantasy Factory. From what Leon told her, Tina had gathered that Anissa was the reason he was in jail in the first place. Tina had warned him long ago about the whores he chose to bring into his life. He'd told her he had it under control, but his reality was proving him wrong. She had stolen his establishment from right under his nose and was running it without issue. It was both admirable and stupid, very stupid, because now Tina had to come clean up the mess. It was her turn to return the favor of freedom to Leon.

Leon gave her the location of the Fantasy Factory, and Tina had posted up in the parking lot for two days, waiting for the face she was looking for to step out. She was in disguise, wearing a wig with long bangs and sunglasses. She thought about trying to go inside but remembered it was members only. So instead she waited patiently.

When finally she saw CoCo exit the building and drive off in her car in a hurry, Tina followed her. She didn't care if she had to ram her car into a ditch, Tina was going to get her one way or another. Luckily, she didn't have to use the ditch idea. CoCo stopped at a restaurant, and Tina parked her car in an alley across the street. Grabbing her purse, Tina hurried across the intersection to where CoCo's blue Toyota was and tried the back door. She smiled when it opened and she got inside. Tina snatched the wig and glasses off her head because when CoCo came back, she wanted to be recognized. It didn't take long for CoCo to get back to the car, and when she did, she was so focused on eating her food that she didn't even feel the presence of another person inside it with her. But when she did, it was like she saw a ghost.

"Hi, Tina," CoCo stammered with wide eyes.

"Don't 'hi, Tina' me, bitch," Tina said and pulled a small handgun out of her bag. She pointed it at the back of CoCo's head. "What's going on with my son?"

"He's in jail. One of the girls he recruited set him up."

"And why haven't you gotten him out yet?"

"I couldn't, Tina. I swear. The girl took all his money. She took all the money in his accounts and all of the money we made for him," CoCo said and then began lying through her teeth. "I've been living in my car and doing what I have to in order to survive without Leon. I miss him so much. I need him. I was gonna save up enough money to bond him out, I swear."

"And how were you gonna do that? By working for Miss Thing? And before you lie again, think twice."

"I . . ." Tina didn't think it was possible for CoCo's eyes to get any bigger, but they did when she realized she was found out. She quickly switched her narrative. "Tina, I didn't have any other choice. I didn't have anywhere to go. Please don't kill me."

"How much money have you made at the club?"

"I don't know."

"Guess!"

"Ten thousand dollars, but Anissa takes out her cut."

"Eight thousand dollars, hmm. And have you put money on Leon's books since he's been locked up?"

"No," CoCo answered honestly.

"Have you gone to see him?"

"No."

"So, if the answer to those questions is no, you really expect me to believe that you were going to bond him out?"

"Tina, I—"

"Shut up!" Tina shouted and pressed the barrel of the gun forcefully on the back of her head. "After my son took you in like a stray dog after you murdered your entire family, this is how you repay him? When you had nothing and nobody, you were just going to let him sit high and dry on his ass to rot."

"I swear I wasn't." CoCo shook her head feverishly, but the truth was already in the air. It was in her actions. Actions that would be punished.

"You know, my concern is definitely my son. However, I am worried about my well-being as well," Tina said and scoffed. "Leon is a good boy. Where his father failed in taking care of me correctly, Leon succeeded tremendously. Because of him I'm able to live lavishly and do whatever it is that I want to do at any given time of the day. But if he's in jail, that means my money stops coming in. Do you get where I'm going with this?"

CoCo's body was frozen stiff in fear, but she gave a tiny nod.

"What did Anissa give you to turn your back on my son?"

"Nothing."

"What did she give you?" Tina repeated.

"Nothing!" CoCo exclaimed with a trembling bottom lip. "After Leon went to jail, she took everything from us. I had no choice but to work for her."

"Why didn't you kill her?"

"What?" CoCo asked as if what Tina had just proposed was the most preposterous thing she'd ever heard.

"Why is Anissa still breathing if she betrayed Leon like that? One would think that you of all people would seek revenge."

"I can't murder someone."

"Why not? It's not like you haven't already done it." Tina stared coldly into CoCo's eyes through the mirror. "No matter. Leon will get his business and his girls back when I'm through here. And me? I'm going to go back to living my good ol' carefree life again."

"How, if he's in jail and Anissa is the new person in charge?"

"I already have that all figured out, but I need your help," Tina told her and lowered her gun.

CoCo let out the air that was in her chest when she felt the pressure of the gun leave the back of her head. "Anything," she said eagerly. "I'll do anything to help daddy."

"Good. I'll be sure to let him know that when he's looking for someone to replace you."

"Replace me?"

What CoCo couldn't see was that the only reason Tina had lowered the weapon was to screw a silencer to the gun. What she didn't know was that Tina did need her help. However, she didn't need her alive to get it. There was a small pfft when Tina fired a bullet into the back of CoCo's skull, splattering blood everywhere in the car. She was dead before her head hit the steering wheel. Before placing the wig and sunglasses back on, Tina snapped a picture of CoCo lying slumped with her eyes still wide open. Once she was satisfied with the photo, she got out of the car and casually crossed the street. She didn't know how long it would take for someone to find CoCo's dead body, but she didn't really care. She had all that she needed.

She felt no remorse for taking a life. In fact, Tina felt nothing at all. CoCo was just an obstacle on the way to the goal. Before dealing with Laron, Tina had been the sweetest girl. But after suffering his abuse, she turned into a monster. He had used up all the sweetness in her and turned it dark. He turned her into a survivor. When she stabbed him after he'd beaten her nearly to death, it had exalted her. He had been the monster under her bed and her demon in the night. Seeing him lying helpless on the ground had made her feel the strongest she'd ever felt. And after he died, there was nothing in the world that put fear in her heart ever again.

Tina didn't even feel the smile on her face when she reached the alley. She snatched the sunglasses and wig off once more and tossed them into the dumpster she was parked by. She had one more thing to do before the day was up. She got in her milk white Mercedes and glanced in the visor mirror at her rustled natural braids.

"I need to get my hair done," she said and laughed sinisterly before pulling off.

Chapter 18

"Shit!" Anissa moaned loudly as fireworks went off behind her eyelids.

Her body quivered as her vaginal wall throbbed around the thing invading them until the sensation was over. She was still breathing heavily when she finally opened her eyes to see the person who had given her such a divine feeling. Kendall grinned down at her right before planting three soft kisses on her lips.

"That's what happens when I don't get to see you," he told her and rolled from on top of her.

"Then maybe I should go a few days without seeing you more often." She gave him a cunning grin of her own and propped her head up on her arm.

The two were entangled in the blankets on Anissa's bed. She'd invited him over to her house because she missed him. She'd moved out from Brynn's condo a while ago, and it was a beautiful thing to have her own home. She and Kendall had made love all throughout the place before ending up in the bedroom.

"Oh, you don't want to do that. I might stalk you," he teased.

"You won't have to." Anissa leaned in toward him and kissed his chin. "I'm sorry I've been missing in action, baby. Things have just been busy at the club."

"The titty bar, you mean," Kendall said, giving her a knowing look.

"Don't do that," Anissa sighed, not wanting to get him started.

"I'm just calling it like it is." Kendall lay back on his back.

Anissa and Kendall had started dating a short time after Leon had gone to jail. She finally used his number and allowed him to take her out to dinner. One date turned into two, and two had turned into ten. Before she knew it, Kendall was her boyfriend, and she had fallen in love. He made her feel things no other man had ever made her feel. The only bad thing was that he hated her job. He didn't know what all went on inside the Fantasy Factory. He just thought it was a strip club. He hated the thought of her being around horny men all day, which was a reason why she never told him about her past. She just wanted to move forward without looking back.

"Baby, I didn't invite you to my place to have this conversation again. Can we please not do this tonight?" she asked in a pleading voice. "I'm the owner, not a dancer. And plus, you don't see me saying anything about you being a personal trainer. I know not all of your clients are old ladies with bad knees."

"Touché, but that still doesn't mean I like the Fantasy Factory. You won't even let me get a membership."

"Because the only pussy you need to see is between my legs." She winked.

"You have a point there," Kendall said.

Anissa smiled, but as she got lost in her own thoughts, her smile faded. There was another reason why she had invited Kendall over, and it wasn't just that she missed his kisses. The next morning was a day she'd been awaiting for a while: Leon's trial. It was the day that he would for sure get locked away for years to come. All Brynn had to do was get on the stand and identify him as her shooter.

"You okay?" Kendall asked, noticing the troubled look on her face.

"Yeah, I'm good."

"No, you're not," he said, calling her on her bluff. "You're thinking about tomorrow, aren't you?"

"How'd you know?"

"It's a big day. It's the day your cousin's shooter gets brought to justice. Is she ready?"

"She says she is." Anissa nodded.

"I wonder what would make a dude do that in the first place," Kendall said, shaking his head.

Anissa grew quiet again. She'd never told him the parameters of her dealings with Leon. She felt that it would just complicate things between them. She felt the less that he knew, the better. Plus, when it was all over, it would be nothing but a bump in the past.

Brynn hummed to herself as she locked the doors to Groove. It was late, but she'd lost track of time counting supplies and restocking. Since she'd been back, she never missed a beat with her business. She felt like she had to make up for lost time. And that she had. Business had been booming so much that she had to hire two more stylists. She also now had an aesthetician, a beautician, and a nail tech in the Groove Salon. The boutique was still doing well, too. She'd just hired a new manager, but she also still got Anissa's input on inventory. Their lives had taken major turns, but they were happy. And that was what mattered the most.

Brynn made her way to the brand-new dark-tinted gray G-Wagen she'd just upgraded to and dug for her keys at the bottom of her Prada bag. All she wanted to do was get home and prep for the next morning. It was a big day. She was going to testify against her shooter. It was crazy that the trial date was finally there. It seemed like it had taken forever and come so fast at the same time. But she was ready to lock him away forever. What he had done to her was take her peace of mind. For the longest time, Brynn was scared to be in the shop by herself. Every time someone would open the door and she would hear the chime, she would jump. It took a while, but eventually she was able to get back to a normal life.

She reached her vehicle just as she found her key fob. Before she could unlock the doors, she saw someone walking up to her out of the corner of her eye. She quickly placed her hand back in her purse and wrapped her hand around her pistol before whipping her head to the right. Some of the tension left her body when she saw that it was a woman in her mid to late forties. Still, she didn't let go of her gun.

"Oh, dang, I must have just missed you." The woman smacked her lips and looked defeated.

"Yeah, we closed an hour ago," Brynn told her. "But if you want, you can call us and schedule an appointment in the morning."

"Are you sure you can't get me in?" the woman asked and removed the hat that she was wearing, revealing some frizzy braids. "I just need two feed-ins. Please can you help me out?"

"I'm sorry. I can't." Brynn shrugged her shoulders apologetically. "I have somewhere very important to be in the morning. I need to get home."

"Maybe you should rethink that."

"Excuse me?" Brynn asked, feeling her patience wearing thin. She didn't understand what the woman didn't understand about the fact that they were closed. But she needed to keep it pushing and do what Brynn had suggested. If she didn't, then she must not have wanted her hair done that badly.

"Testifying tomorrow. You should rethink it," the woman said, and suddenly a sinister smile formed on her lips.

Brynn felt her heart drop to her stomach. "Who are you?"

"Someone here to remind you that Leon's reach still stretches outside of those prison walls. I see you have your life back. If you value it, and those around you, then I would suggest you just stay home tomorrow."

"I can't do that. That man tried to murder me."

"Then, baby, you just murdered your friends. Because their blood will be on your hands. Don't testify, and I'll let you all live. Testify, and I will kill each and every one of you one by one. Including that cousin of yours."

On her last word, the lady walked away and was gone quicker than she'd come. Brynn had been so stunned that she'd forgotten all about the gun in her hand. The woman's aura had been a dark one, and the hair on the back of Brynn's neck were standing up. She tried to shake the words she'd just been told. She was probably just one of Leon's old hoes trying to intimidate her from testifying.

Brynn hurried to unlock her door before someone else popped up trying to scare her. She got inside the G-Wagen and started it so that she could finally go home to her condo. Before she pulled off, an unpleasant aroma hit her nose. She made a face and looked to the passenger seat to see if maybe she'd left some food sitting in the hot car, but there was nothing. Brynn turned her head to look in the back seat to find the source of the smell and instantly started screaming.

She'd found the source of the smell: it was a dead body. Brynn knew she was dead because the back of the woman's head had a huge chunk missing. It was CoCo, one of the girls who worked for Anissa. Her entire body shook as she fumbled to open the door again, and she fell to the ground. She sobbed and choked as she threw up everything in her stomach. She didn't need to question who was responsible for putting the body there. Brynn had received the message loud and clear.

"A man accused of attempted murder walked free this morning after the witness never showed up to court. There are no details on why this happened, but what we do know is that he is a free man."

Listening to it was almost worse than watching it happen live. That morning was the day that was supposed to bring peace to her life, but instead it caused Anissa more grief. Leon was supposed to have gotten twenty years in prison that day. However, Brynn never showed up to court, leaving Anissa standing there looking a fool. She would never forget the self-satisfied expression on Leon's face when the judge was forced to throw the case out. He was a free man. Anissa was happy that they were in such a public place because the look Leon shot her sent chills down her spine. She could only imagine the things going through his head.

After court, the only thing on Anissa's mind was to find Detective Evans in the courtroom. He was just as flabbergasted as Anissa. There had been no doubt in either of their minds that Leon was going to be found guilty.

"What the hell just happened? Where the fuck is Brynn?" he asked her.

"I don't know," she answered, looking him in his angry eyes. "She said she was gonna be here."

"Well, she isn't."

"I see that," Anissa sighed in a defeated fashion. "So, what's next?"

"There is no 'next.' He's a free man."

"But certainly there is something you can do. He tried to kill her. You already have her statement."

"But we needed her testimony to nail him. And since we don't have that, the son of a bitch walks free."

"No." Anissa shook her head. "How did this happen?"

"Intimidation maybe," Detective Evans guessed. "But honestly there could be a number of reasons why Brynn didn't show up today. It's not so uncommon with witnesses. Sometimes the fear gets the best of them."

"That's not Brynn," Anissa said.

"Then maybe you should ask her why yourself." Detective Evans patted her on the shoulder, and with one last disappointed nod, he walked away.

He was right. She needed to find Brynn. She knew how important it was to put Leon away. Why had she not done the one thing she was supposed to do? Not only because he had shot her, but now Anissa was going to be the number one person on his hit list.

Anissa left the courthouse and went to Brynn's condo. The entire ride she was paranoid and constantly checking her rearview mirror. It was something she was sure would be her new normal. It wasn't a question of *if* Leon would come for her, but *when*.

Once she got to Brynn's house, she barely parked before hopping out and rushing up to her cousin's floor. She didn't even realize until she reached for her phone at Brynn's door that she'd left her purse in the car.

"Brynn!" Anissa called out. "Brynn, are you in there?"

She banged on the door with her palms before she remembered she knew the code. Or at least she thought she did. It had been a while since she'd been to Brynn's, and she hoped she hadn't change it. Anissa tried Brynn's birthday, and sure enough it worked.

"Brynn!" Anissa shouted when she pushed open the door.

She didn't need to shout, because she found Brynn sitting right at the island in her kitchen. Anissa was so shocked to see her sitting there so casually that she just stood there holding the door open. It was apparent that Brynn had been crying. Her eyes were puffy, and she looked like she hadn't gotten any sleep the night before.

"Brynn, where were you today? He walked free. Leon walked free!"

"You shouldn't have come here," Brynn told her, disregarding everything Anissa had just said. "You really shouldn't have come here, Nissa."

"What the fuck do you mean I shouldn't have come here?" Anissa asked wide-eyed, finally letting the door close.

"Because now you're about to die," a voice Anissa didn't recognize said from behind her.

Anissa whipped around and stood face-to-face with a woman she didn't recognize. The woman was older, but she was very beautiful. She had a timeless look about her. Anissa didn't know her, but the woman was looking at her like she knew who she was. Anissa's eyes whipped from the woman to Brynn and then back to the woman.

"Who the hell are you?"

"She's the reason I didn't come today. Anissa, she killed CoCo," Brynn stammered.

"She what?" Anissa's eyes grew wide at the woman's malicious smile.

"She killed her and put her in my car. And then she forced me to take her here. We've been here since last night."

"CoCo is dead?" Anissa said, trying to comprehend what she'd just been told.

"From what I've heard about you, I thought you would be smarter, Anissa," the woman said.

"Who are you? And how the hell do you know my name?"

"Oh, how rude of me. I never introduced myself," she said, the smile frozen on her face. "I'm Tina, the mother of the man whose life you tried to take. And we're here to take it back."

"We?"

"Leon is on his way. And when he gets here, you'll have some explaining to do."

"Do you think I'm just gonna stay here and wait for him? Come on, Brynn," Anissa said and reached for her cousin. "Let's go."

Brynn didn't budge. Instead she looked at Tina, causing Anissa to follow her gaze. Tina had a gun pointed at them and was shaking her head.

"Do *you* think I won't use this? I can't kill you yet, Anissa, but your cousin? I've gotten my use out of her already."

Tina cocked the gun and made to point it at Brynn.

"No!" Anissa shouted and put her body in between Tina and Brynn. "What is it that you want?"

"I just want to go back to my regular life that you so rudely interrupted by cutting my son's cash flow off. *He* wants back everything you stole from him. Minus CoCo, but she was disloyal. She had that coming to her."

"If you hurt us, they'll know it was Leon who did it." Anissa tried to make her voice sound confident. "He just got out of jail and we turn up dead? That would be too easy."

Tina stared blankly at her for a few moments before breaking out into a slow laugh. It ended with her bellowing loudly, like Anissa had told the joke of the century. The faint sound of a phone vibrating sounded, and Tina pulled a flip phone from the pocket of her formfitting jeans. She read something on the screen, and her eyes lit up.

"He's on the way," she told them.

Chapter 19

It had been a year since Leon had been face-to-face with Anissa, and when he reached the location Tina had sent him, the look on his face was priceless. He was satisfied with Tina's handiwork because she had single-handedly gotten him released and exonerated. She'd been holding both Brynn and Anissa at gunpoint, kneeling with their hands on their heads, when she opened the door for him.

"Hey, son," Tina said and kissed him on the cheek. "How was the ride over?"

"Exciting. I'm a free man. Have you had your fun with them yet?" he asked and nodded his head toward where Brynn and Anissa were kneeling.

"I had my fun last night," she said and then made a concerned face. "I had to kill CoCo. She was working for *her*."

One would have thought that Leon would have felt a pinch of something. After all, CoCo had been Leon's oldest and most loyal girl. But while he was locked up, she hadn't visited him once. She wasn't that loyal. Whatever Tina had done to her, he hoped that it hurt.

"I'll have ten more CoCos in no time," he said, pulling his gun from his waist before he approached Anissa. He got down on her eye level and spat in her face. "You tried to end me. How does it feel to be where you are now?"

"Pretty good. I became the person you dreamed of becoming," she answered boldly.

"Is that right?" Leon scoffed, and before she could say another smart remark, he slapped her hard across the face with his gun. He hit her so hard that she fell over, and Brynn cried out in distress. "Bitch! I should have known you could never be trained."

"You . . ." Anissa spat the blood in her mouth to the ground as she caught her breath. "You can't kill me. They'll know you did it."

"Duh, what do you think I am, stupid? I'm not gon' kill you." An ominous smile spread on his lips. "Not until you sign these papers anyways."

From his back pocket he pulled a small, folded stack of papers. He unfolded them and shoved them into her face. They were the same papers she'd tricked him into signing a year ago, except his were unsigned. He'd had them sent to him while he was locked up, and he looked at them every day in hopes that he would be able to get his revenge. He wouldn't be able to recover the money she stole from him, but he could make it back.

"I'm not signing those. The Fantasy Factory is mine. The girls are mine. And when I die, it will all be mine. I don't care what you do to me. I'll never give it to you," Anissa told him.

"Even if I"—Leon dropped the papers in front of Anissa and snatched Brynn up by her hair—"kill your cousin? And this time I'll be sure to put two bullets in her skull."

He put his gun to Brynn's head and stood up with her. He could feel her heart rate accelerate, and her fear excited him.

"Anissa!"

"Brynn!" Anissa shouted, the tough-girl act instantly diminishing. Tears welled in her eyes seeing the gun against Brynn's temple. "No, don't hurt her."

"Sign the papers then."

"You'll kill us both if I do."

"Nah." Leon shook his head. "I have something special planned for you. I never got to make a dollar off that sweet pussy between your legs."

"No." Anissa shook her head. "I'd rather die."

"I see you need a little more persuasion," Leon said and cocked his gun.

He applied pressure to the trigger, but right before he could put a bullet in Brynn's head, she jerked her head back forcefully into his nose. The sudden pain came at such a shock that he dropped the gun right in front of Anissa. She made a quick grab for it and jumped to her feet. She aimed her gun to shoot Leon, but in the heat of the moment, she had forgotten all about Tina.

Boom!

Tina's bullet entered Anissa's side with a small splatter of blood. Anissa fell back into the island and clutched the entrance point of the bullet. Before she fell to the ground, she let off a shot of her own, and the bullet seemed to go in slow motion. It passed Leon and Brynn, traveled all the way to Tina, and went right through her eye and out the back of her head. Her neck snapped back from the force of the bullet, and the gun in her hand dropped before her body did.

"Tina!"

Leon's shout was deafening, and he let Brynn go to rush to her side. He lifted her lifeless body into his arms and shook her gently. When she didn't move, he shook her again.

"Tina?" he asked in a disbelieving tone. When she didn't respond, he clutched her to his chest. "No!"

His sob got caught in his throat and came out as an earth-shattering scream. Anissa had taken away everything that meant something to him. The rage he felt was bigger than his body, and he felt like he was about to explode. His eyes fell on Tina's gun, and he reached for it with all intentions of emptying the clip.

"I wouldn't do that if I were you," Anissa's voice sounded.

He looked toward her and saw that she had struggled back to her feet. Brynn was standing beside her, glaring at Leon. Anissa was shaky, but she had his gun pointed right at him. Softly, Leon laid Tina's body down and got to his feet.

"You won't kill me."

"How are you so sure?"

"Because you're weak!" Leon shouted and took a step toward her. "You should have killed me when you found out I was the one who tried to kill your cousin. But you didn't, because you're weak! You took everything from me! But you will never be me."

"You know what, Leon? I'm better than you."

On her last word, Leon leaped for her throat, and she pulled the trigger one last time. At first, he thought she'd missed, but then he realized that he couldn't breathe or swallow. He staggered backward, and his hands flew to his neck in dismay. When he withdrew and looked down at them, he saw that they were covered in blood. Leon had a hole in his neck. That wasn't how the day was supposed to go. Leon was supposed to have left jail and gotten his club back. Instead he'd gotten the only woman he loved killed, and he would be following soon. He tried to reach for Anissa, but his body was giving out on him. He dropped to his knees, knowing that he would be dead in seconds. His last visual was of Anissa flipping him off.

Anissa clutched her side and let the smoking gun fall to her side. She stared at Leon's still body to make sure it was down for the count. But the bullet in the middle of his neck should have ensured that. There was no coming back from that. Tina's body wasn't too far away from him, and their blood had started to swirl together. Anissa's eyes blurred for a second, and then the pain came.

"Ugh," she groaned as her legs gave out under her.

"I got you." Brynn caught her before her knees hit the ground, and she held her back up. "You're losing a lot of blood, but if I survived three gunshots, you can survive one."

Anissa didn't know how Brynn had made it out of that, because the burning sensation coming from her side was too much to bear. She didn't have the energy to walk, but she had to. With Brynn's help, she stepped over the two dead bodies and out of the condo.

"Brynn," Anissa finally said weakly when they were on the elevator, "if I live, can you check on my girls when we get to the hospital?"

"You're not gonna die. It looks like you just have a flesh wound," Brynn reassured her. "You're feeling weak because you're losing blood. As far as the club, I'm sure Harmony has everything on lock right now. We were just almost murdered. That makes two times for me. Behind *your* shit!"

"I'm sorry," Anissa said and grimaced at the pain in her side. "If I haven't told you recently, I love you. And I'm sorry about all of this. I never meant for it to happen."

"Shh. Save your strength," Brynn said a little more softly. "And I know you didn't."

Anissa was going in and out of consciousness. One minute she was on the elevator, and the next she was outside on a stretcher. One of Brynn's neighbors had heard the gunshots and called 911.

"Load her on and get her to the hospital stat! She's losing blood fast," Anissa heard an EMT shout while she lay on her back looking at the blue sky. She then heard that same voice ask a question. "Are you going with her, ma'am?"

"Yes," Brynn answered. "Can I ride with her?"

"Of course."

"We have another live one inside!"

Those words were yelled by someone in the distance and caused everyone around them to move in a frenzy. Anissa's heart felt like it froze over because it was impossible. She thought it was over. She'd killed Tina and Leon, so who was alive? Brynn wasn't paying attention to what was going on around her. She was only focused on her cousin. Anissa used the little strength she had left to turn her head as they wheeled her to the ambulance. Right before they lifted her inside, she was able to see another body wheeled out on a stretcher. It didn't have a cover over it, so she knew the person was alive.

"We have a male! Late twenties. Get him on a stretcher now!" the same voice shouted urgently. "He has a bullet in his neck. We can save him, but we have to move quick!"

"No," Anissa whispered right as the EMT slammed the doors shut.

To Be Continued